"I don't think people cont... should say good-night."

Lacy swallowed. "You don't?"

"Nope. I think it's more like this." Morgan clamped an arm around her waist and swooped her up against the solid wall of his body. Then he bent his head and planted his mouth squarely over hers.

Morgan kissed the way he did everything else—in a straight, no-nonsense manner that hit Lacy like the force of a two-ton bull. She opened her mouth under his. It had been some time since she'd kissed a man. She'd almost forgotten what it felt like to be pressed against a hard, masculine body, to have a man's lips travel over hers.

More, she thought vaguely. She wanted more. She thrust her hips forward. He moved his thigh, inserting it between her legs. She gasped pleasure into his mouth and clutched him tighter, using her tongue to get a better taste of him, moving herself against him.

Suddenly Morgan released her. "We'd better stop that, honey, or your dad will be out here with a shotgun."

It wasn't her father's shotgun he had to worry about. If he kissed her like that again, she might go after him with one herself—only it wouldn't be marriage she had in mind.

This story was inspired by the mention of a lonely cowboy in Temptation #551, *The Last Hero*. **Alyssa Dean** didn't plan on writing Morgan's story, but a number of people, including the author's children, were worried about Morgan Brillings and felt badly that he was by himself. When the family started discussing what he was going to do at Christmas, Alyssa knew it was past time to act. She wrote this romance about sexy cowboy Morgan Brillings so he wouldn't be alone—and so her family could stop worrying about him!

Don't miss Alyssa's next book in Harlequin's new series, Harlequin Duets, in July 1999!

Books by Alyssa Dean

HARLEQUIN TEMPTATION
524—MAD ABOUT YOU
551—THE LAST HERO
636—RESCUING CHRISTINE

HARLEQUIN LOVE & LAUGHTER
33—MISTLETOE MISCHIEF

Don't miss any of our special offers. Write to us at the following address for information on our newest releases.

Harlequin Reader Service
U.S.: 3010 Walden Ave., P.O. Box 1325, Buffalo, NY 14269
Canadian: P.O. Box 609, Fort Erie, Ont. L2A 5X3

HER DESPERADO
Alyssa Dean

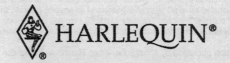

HARLEQUIN®

TORONTO • NEW YORK • LONDON
AMSTERDAM • PARIS • SYDNEY • HAMBURG
STOCKHOLM • ATHENS • TOKYO • MILAN • MADRID
PRAGUE • WARSAW • BUDAPEST • AUCKLAND

For Aileen and Warren
with special thanks to
Rod, Robbie, Vern and Paul

ISBN 0-373-25819-4

HER DESPERADO

Copyright © 1999 by Patsy McNish.

1

"HOW ABOUT A HANDSOME, mysterious stranger?" Lacy suggested. She spliced the break in the barbed-wire fence with a pair of pliers. "Maybe that's exactly what we need around here, Oscar. A handsome, mysterious stranger."

Oscar, a red-and-white Border collie, tilted his head to one side and gave her a quizzical look.

Lacy rested back on her heels, pulled off one of her heavy leather work gloves and swiped an arm across her sweat-dampened brow. "You know the type I mean. The ones that show up in movies just as the young, beautiful rancher's daughter is about to lose her ranch." She stared into the distance now dimming in the twilight. "She's at her wit's end. There's no water. The cattle are dying. The wicked creditors are demanding their money. The situation looks hopeless." She glanced down at Oscar. "Sounds an awful lot like real life, doesn't it?"

He tipped his head to the other side and whined.

"Not exactly like real life," Lacy amended. "Our situation isn't hopeless."

Granted, it was getting darn close to being that way. Their entire hay crop had burned, forcing them to buy feed for the winter. Their best bull, along with a large number of heifers had broken through the fence and drowned in the rain-swollen creek. The combine had broken down, requiring extensive, and expensive, repairs. Their finances were in a dangerous state, and unless things improved dramatically, they were going to be in a real mess.

"In the movies when that happens, a great-looking guy with no name and a veiled past rides into town. He falls for the daughter. She falls for him. They have a wild and passionate romance, which includes a lot of hot and heavy sex, and he ends up saving her ranch from the hordes of creditors."

Oscar flopped to the ground beside her and yawned.

Lacy gave his head a pat. "You don't think there's much chance of that happening around here, do you?"

Oscar closed his eyes and put his head on his paws. Lacy pushed herself up and took a look around. The hill she was standing on gave her a panoramic view of the area. Apart from the few trees on her left and the creek at the bottom of the small valley, there was nothing to see but green grass, barbed-wire fences and Red Angus cattle. Other than her shadow, there wasn't another human being in sight—certainly no imaginary hero.

Lacy bent to retrieve the tools she'd been using to mend the fence. "You could be right, Oscar. There haven't been more than half a dozen strangers show up in Silver Spurs all year, much less out here. None of those was good-looking, and they certainly weren't here to help out a rancher's daughter. They were mostly people who got off the interstate by accident and wanted to get back on."

Her dog looked as bored as those people had.

Lacy packed her pliers, sidecutters, splicing wire and gloves into the saddlebag of one of the two horses standing nearby.

"And except for the rancher's-daughter part, I don't qualify for the heroine position. Twenty-eight can hardly be considered young and I wouldn't call myself beautiful." She looked down at her mud-encrusted jeans and grimaced. "Most of the time I can't even call myself clean."

Most of the time she didn't call herself anything. She was too busy in the mornings to do much more than slip on jeans and a shirt, then run a comb through her hair. As for makeup, well, every so often she put on a little lipstick, although she couldn't remember the last time she'd done even that. What was the point? She didn't need to look glamorous to mend fences, take care of cattle or bale hay.

"The only way he's going to fall for me is if he prefers the back-to-nature type," she decided.

That seemed unlikely. Men preferred leggy blondes, not short brunettes who smelled more like horses and hay than perfume. Still, it was *her* fantasy. She could imagine anyone she wanted to imagine. She conjured up a great-looking guy riding up the hill and spotting her. "Wonderful!" he'd exclaim. "I've always been attracted to back-to-nature types. How about if we have a hot romance and I save your ranch for you?"

Lacy giggled at the image. She'd say, "Of course you can, Mr. Stranger." They'd have a torrid affair and then he'd... He'd what? She slapped the saddlebag closed. "Even if he did show up, what could he do?" she asked Oscar. "In the movies, he'd shoot the wicked creditors, but we don't have any of those.

They aren't really wicked. They just want the money we owe them." She thought for a moment. "Unless his saddlebags were loaded with gold, my hero couldn't do much."

She made a face. Terrific. Now she needed a rich, handsome, mysterious stranger who liked the back-to-nature type. She squinted into the distance. No wonder this guy didn't show. He probably didn't exist!

Lacy gave the horse a pat on the withers and wandered over to the lead horse. "It's best if he doesn't show up. If he did materialize and solve all my problems, what would I do with him? The last thing I need is another man around here telling me how to run the place."

She envisioned the house, populated by her mother, her father, herself and Mr. Stranger. Her mother would be bustling around the kitchen, doing mother-type things, while her father and Mr. Stranger discussed the ranch and how best to run it. What would she be doing? Would she be involved in a discussion with the men? Nope, she'd be washing the dishes. And when she finished that, she'd have to listen to those other two telling her what to do. That would drive her around the bend!

She couldn't bear to have another male bossing her around. Her father was hard enough to handle. Oh, he was a wonderful man, and she loved him dearly. However, he had to be the biggest chauvinist this side of the Pacific Ocean. He also had his own ideas about how the ranch was supposed to be run. Lacy didn't blame him. He'd been running this place ever since he'd taken it over from his father and he was used to doing things his own way. Still, she wasn't a complete novice, either. She'd lived here all her life, except for a brief absence when she'd been at agricultural college. She'd pretty much taken over when her father had had a heart attack three years ago, and she did the bulk of the work. Yet her dad insisted on telling her what to do and how to do it. She didn't need another man around to do that, too.

In a vain attempt to clean her hands, she rubbed them together. It could very well be worse than that. Mr. Stranger wouldn't be content with just bossing her around. He'd take over completely! He'd get to do all the fun stuff, like branding and working with the horses and fixing the fences, while she'd be stuck with cooking and cleaning.

That's sure how it was with all of her married friends. They did the dull chores while the men had a good time. Sometimes Lacy found herself wondering why the women had bothered to get married in the first place. There were odd moments when she wished there was more of a masculine presence in her life, but those were few and far between—and usually occurred at a party when she saw a couple snuggling together. "I suppose we could always have a torrid affair," she mused. "Then he could...ride off into the sunset or...something."

That would be perfect. A great-looking, wealthy, mysterious guy...a big romance. Then he would go away and she could still have the ranch to call her own. Of course, carrying on this torrid affair might be something of a problem. After all, she did live with her parents! She couldn't imagine them calmly going about their business while she and a stranger were having wild, illicit sex in her bedroom. They'd have to sneak off into the bushes, which would be cold, uncomfortable and unromantic. There was always the hotel in town, but that wouldn't work. Everyone in Silver Spurs would know about it before they'd gotten past the removing-their-clothes stage. They'd have to drive to the city and check into some sleazy motel—

"Forget it," she ordered herself. There was no point in planning a secret rendezvous with a mystery man who wasn't going to show. She'd be better off planning on a million dollars falling from the sky!

She took a hopeful look upward, but not a single greenback dropped out of the twilit heavens. Apparently that wasn't on today's agenda, either.

Lacy untied the horses and gathered the reins in her hand. Okay, a handsome, mysterious stranger was out. So what? She didn't need a man to solve her problems. She was quite capable of doing that herself. Still, she wouldn't mind an affair with a great-looking guy who was crazy about her. A guy who would at least help her find a solution.

She daydreamed a few more minutes, then pushed the notion aside and put a foot in the stirrup. "Come on, Oscar. If we hurry, we can make it back before..."

Her voice trailed off as she glanced at the dog. Oscar was no longer lying passively at her feet. Instead, he was standing at full attention, staring toward a clump of trees on their left. Lacy turned to see what he was looking at, then froze.

It was a man. He was standing about fifty yards away on the other side of the fence, just outside the trees. From the tip of his worn brown cowboy hat to the toes of his scuffed boots he was the picture of the man she'd just been daydreaming about. He was over six feet tall, with a brown mustache and an unshaven chin. He was wearing brown pants, brown leather chaps and a dusty-looking brown oilskin. A leather holster was wrapped around his narrow waist while one shoulder held a battered saddlebag. He was mysterious enough and handsome enough to fulfill every fantasy Lacy had *ever* had.

For a moment, he stared at her across the expanse of grass and deepening shadows. Then he tipped the brim of his hat, turned on his heel and moseyed into the trees.

Lacy gaped at the place he'd just been, while her heart rate settled back to normal. Had she just imagined that, or had someone really been there?

She gave her head a shake. She hadn't imagined anything. There had been a man there—a man she'd never seen before. What could he be doing in this neck of the woods? This small valley was located on the southwestern edge of their ranch, with a shallow creek dividing it from their neighbor's property. The only access was by horseback, and the only reason to come here was to check on the cattle or fix the fences.

So why had that guy suddenly turned up?

Lacy moistened her lips. She shouldn't just let a stranger wander around out here. He could be lost, and need some help, although he didn't look like the type who needed any. Still, she ought to find out what he was doing in these parts—and get a chance to at least introduce herself. "You stay here, Oscar," she ordered. "Watch the horses."

Oscar looked at her, then back to the trees before woofing once.

She looped the reins around the fence post and climbed through the barbed-wire fence.

MORGAN BRILLINGS REINED his black horse to a halt at the top of the hill and peered through the darkening shadows toward the other side of the creek. He couldn't see anyone, but he recognized the two horses—the gray gelding the Johnsons used as a packhorse, and Lacy's rusty-colored quarter horse, the one she called Intrigue. Morgan had no idea why. Intrigue was a decent enough animal, but there wasn't a whole lot intriguing about him.

He hesitated for a moment, then urged his horse down the hill. He'd spent the day on his own, checking his fences and his cattle. There was nothing waiting for him back home except an empty house. He was used to his own company, but he wouldn't mind spending a minute or two talking with Lacy.

A few years ago, he wouldn't have considered seeking out other people, he thought as he forded the stream. He'd have been too preoccupied with his ranch, his cattle, his horses... Recently, though, he'd found himself making plans to see other human beings. Every couple of days he made some excuse to drive into town or drop by to visit a neighbor—and his morning chats with his hired hand covered a lot more than the daily list of things to do. This surprising desire to socialize puzzled Morgan even while he was doing it. It could be that he was just reacting to a couple of exceptionally long, unnaturally cold winters. Or it could be that his brother was right, and he was lonely.

His brother, Wade, had left the ranch at a young age, and for years they'd seen little of each other. Over the past few months, that had changed. Wade had taken to phoning once a week. He was also stopping by on a more frequent basis.

Morgan knew the reason for Wade's unusual behavior. It was that cute little Canadian bride of his. Morgan had been stunned when Wade phoned to announce that he was getting married. He'd been even more stunned when he met the woman. Cassie was a sweet little thing, but she was an odd choice for a man like Wade. She wasn't much of a cook, she owned more clothes than most folks in North America put together, and she talked endlessly about incomprehensible subjects like decor and wardrobes. Last time they came for a visit, she'd insisted on recovering his living-room furniture and nagged Wade and Morgan into repainting the place.

According to Wade, Cassie was typical of all women. "They just go around doing peculiar, illogical things," Wade had explained while Cassie was studying paint samples. "I think it's got something to do with their hormones."

Morgan had nodded agreement, although privately he doubted his brother knew much about hormones...or anything else to do with the opposite sex. He and Wade had been raised by their father after their mother died. Wade had left at a young age to join the navy, while Morgan had remained on the ranch. Neither one of them could honestly be classified as experts on female behavior. Ranching hadn't given Morgan either the time or the opportunity to learn much about women, and he didn't think female psychology had played a major role in Wade's naval career. Besides, although "peculiar" and "illogical" certainly described Wade's wife, it didn't describe all women.

Take Lacy for example. Morgan had known Lacy all his life, and she was nothing like Wade's wife. He'd never seen her fuss over her short brown hair, put makeup on her tanned, freckled face or concern herself about what she wore. Her conversation revolved around cattle and weather, not clothes and paint colors. That wasn't too surprising. Lacy had been working on the Johnson ranch since she was little, and now pretty much ran the place. She was doing a decent job of it, too—at least, she had until this year. This year, the Johnsons had run into a streak of bad luck like Morgan had never seen before. He hoped that was all behind them now.

He stopped his horse beside the other two. They ignored him, their attention fixed on a grove of trees a short distance away. Morgan eyed them as he dismounted, aware of a growing sense of unease. It was too quiet, the animals were acting a mite strange, and there was still no sign of Lacy.

He bent to scratch the dog behind the ears. "Hey, Oscar, what's going on? Where's Lacy?"

The dog whined and looked back at the trees. Morgan peered in the direction his long shadow was making toward the outcropping. He couldn't see anything, but according to the critters, there was something going on over there.

He strode toward them. He'd almost reached the edge of the grove when the branches exploded outward, followed by a woman. It was Lacy, her head bare, her wavy brown hair flying behind her. She streaked toward him, her attention on where she'd been, not where she was going. Before Morgan could react, she barreled right into him.

Morgan put a hand on her shoulder to steady her from the impact. She looked up at him, gasped, then tried to wrench herself out of his grasp. Morgan instinctively tightened his grip. "Cut it out, Lacy."

Lacy froze and gaped up at him. There was still enough light for him to make out the paleness of her face and the terror in her green eyes. "M-Morgan?"

"Yeah. I—"

"Oh, Morgan," she breathed. She glanced over her shoulder, toward the trees. Then, to his utter astonishment, she threw herself against him. "Oh, Morgan, Morgan. I am so glad you're here."

Morgan raised his hand and stroked it down her back. He could feel her tremble under his palm. Her arms closed around his waist, her breasts pressed against his chest, and an unexpected warmth pooled in the lower regions of his body. He cleared his throat. "What's going on?"

"Back there." She took another apprehensive look over her shoulder. "There was a…a…a…"

Morgan made a swift mental list of all the things that could happen to a lone human out here. "A what? Cougar? Grizzly?"

She shook her head. "No."

"Then what?" Morgan peered over her head, trying to see through the tree branches. He thought about the Winchester in the rifle holster on his horse, then figured he'd better hold her a while longer.

"A ghost." Lacy raised her head, her face pale, her green eyes wide open. "Oh my God, Morgan, I've just seen a ghost."

"ONE MINUTE HE WAS THERE," Lacy concluded, "standing on the other side of the trees right beside a pile of rocks. And then...then he...disappeared." She shuddered as she recalled the scene. The sunlight fading. The cowboy standing in front of a large boulder, looking straight at her. She'd opened her mouth to speak to him and... "He made some kind of gesture with his hand. Then...well, then he sort of...of floated apart—almost as if he were made of fog."

She took a sip of tea from the mug in her hand and examined her audience to see how they were taking this. They were seated in her parents' living room. Lacy was on the black leather couch. Her father was in his usual chair on her left, and on her right, in a green-and-gold chair that matched her father's, was Morgan Brillings.

Lacy lowered her eyelashes and studied Morgan from under them. He was typical of the men around here—tall, lean, with black hair that fell over his forehead, deep-set blue eyes in a tanned, craggy face. Yet there was something about him that reminded her of the apparition she'd seen a couple of hours ago.

Shivering, Lacy averted her eyes. That was silly. Morgan was nothing like her handsome, mysterious stranger. Oh, he was good-looking enough, she supposed, but there wasn't anything mysterious about him. She'd known him all her life. He was just their next-door neighbor—more her father's friend than her own.

Besides, she'd never seen him disappear into thin air.

Lacy took another swallow of tea and turned her

attention to her father. Walt Johnson had aged a lot since his heart attack. His hair was almost completely white now and the lines in his face had deepened. It was a good thing he hadn't seen what she had. That wouldn't have done his heart one bit of good.

He exchanged a look with Morgan, then frowned over at Lacy. "You shouldn't have followed that character in the first place, Lacy. You should've gotten the hell out of there."

Lacy shook her head. "There was no reason for me to run off! Besides, he was a stranger on our property. I had to find out what he was doing there." Apart from that, when a girl wished for a handsome, mysterious stranger and one made an appearance, she couldn't just ignore him. "I'm sure you would've done exactly the same."

"I may have," her father allowed. "But that's a different thing. *You* are a woman."

"Oh, Dad!" Lacy dropped her head back against the couch. Her being female hadn't stopped her from handling things around here when her father had been unable to. She mended fences, branded cattle, hauled around bales of hay...she'd even repaired the engine on the tractor. But every so often, when it was most convenient for him and least convenient for her, her father remembered that he had a daughter instead of a son!

She opened her mouth to argue, then closed it again. Come to think of it, her gender had a lot to do with why she'd followed that man.

"I didn't know he was a ghost. Maybe if I had, I wouldn't have followed him." It was such a shame. The best-looking man she'd seen in ages, and he turned out to be from another dimension. Why couldn't he just have been from Texas?

Her father spoke again. "There's no such thing as ghosts."

Lacy had been expecting that, but she still felt defensive. "I didn't think so, either, until I saw one vanish right in front of me."

"Lacy—"

"It had to be a ghost," she insisted. "The only other option is that he was a space alien beaming up to his ship. I think the ghost is a bit more probable."

Walt's gaze met Morgan's. "What about you, Morgan? You see any sign of...anything?"

Morgan shook his head. "Nope. But I didn't get there until after Lacy saw this character. It was getting dark, and I didn't spend much time trying to find him." He glanced over at her. "I thought it best if I got Lacy out of there."

He'd certainly done that. He'd insisted on her staying with the horses while he took a brief look around. He'd returned a few minutes later, reported that he hadn't seen anything and insisted on accompanying her home.

And she'd let him! Lacy took another sip of tea. Not only had she let him, she'd enjoyed the feeling of being protected. What was the matter with her? First she'd thrown herself at Morgan, then she'd liked having him take care of her. Did seeing a ghost turn everyone into a wimp or was it just her?

Morgan spoke again. "It could be that this guy saw me coming and took off."

"He didn't take off," Lacy objected. "He disappeared." The men exchanged a look. "He did!" Lacy asserted. She saw the skepticism on their faces and wished her mother was home. She might not believe Lacy any more than the men did, but at least she would have provided some moral support. "I know what I saw! There was a man—or what looked like a man. He disappeared into thin air."

The men exchanged another glance. Lacy got to her feet, positive that if she stayed in this room another minute, she'd shake one or both of them.

"I think I need some more tea," she announced. She snatched up her cup and stomped toward the kitchen. The room behind her settled into silence. Lacy pushed through the swinging kitchen doors, mentally muttering to herself. She shouldn't blame them, she supposed. It didn't sound too likely. Still, she knew what she'd seen.

Her father's voice drifted in from the living room. "I don't know what's gotten into her. She knows darn well there are no such things as ghosts." He sighed heavily. "She must have gotten too much sun."

"I did not get too much sun!" Lacy muttered under her breath. She was no tenderfoot. She knew better than to risk sunstroke!

"I don't know, Walt," Morgan drawled. "She was pretty shook up. Practically threw herself at me."

Lacy's cheeks warmed. What had possessed her to rush into Morgan's arms like that? It wasn't something she usually did. She'd just been so glad to see someone—a human someone, that is—that she'd leaped at him. She had a brief flash of herself landing against him, which brought back a number of other memories—the feeling of his hand soothing on her back, his hard chest under her cheek, his strong thighs pressing into hers.

It hadn't been an unpleasant experience.

That was simply because she'd been frightened. She'd been glad to see another human being, that's all. Anyone would have felt good.

She shoved away the nagging suspicion that she wasn't being entirely honest with herself and listened as Morgan spoke again. "On the other hand, she *is* a woman." Lacy tiptoed to the swinging doors and peeked over them. Morgan was stretching back in his chair, stroking his chin with one hand. "Sometimes they can be a little irrational at times," he continued. "I understand it's got something to do with hormones."

And what would you know about hormones, Morgan Brillings? He didn't spend a lot of time with women—at least, Lacy didn't recall seeing him with any. Then again, she hadn't made much of an effort to notice. He was a decent-looking man. He probably had some experience in that area, although she—

You have just seen a ghost, Lacy scolded herself. *It's no time to be wondering about Morgan Brillings's dating habits.* Instead, she concentrated on the conversation.

"That's true," Walt was saying. "Her mother can be like that."

Her mother? Lacy put a hand over her mouth to hold in a giggle. Her mother was the most dependable person on the face of the earth. The most erratic thing she did was occasionally wash clothes on Monday afternoon instead of Monday morning.

Morgan spoke again. "Even so, I'd say Lacy saw something out there, although I'm not sure what it was."

Walt was silent for a moment while he considered that. "I don't know what anyone would have been doing up there, Morgan—unless she caught sight of a rustler. I hear there's been a bit of rustling going on up near Billings. Could be that they've moved down here."

"Could be," Morgan agreed.

"That's ridiculous," Lacy whispered. "Ghosts do not steal livestock." Her man had been dressed like someone who knew his way around cattle and horses—but he'd also pulled that disappearing act. If rustlers could do that, they'd make a fortune in the circus and wouldn't need to steal cows!

"Maybe we should give Dwight Lanigan a call," Walt suggested.

Lacy rolled her eyes at that. Dwight was the sheriff. What did they think the sheriff was going to do? Put together a posse and go ghost hunting? Come to think of it, that's probably exactly what the sheriff would do!

She decided the men had spent enough time discussing the situation behind her back and pushed through the swinging doors into the living room. "There's no need for the sheriff."

The men looked over at her, then back at each other. "Lacy's right," Morgan decided. "There's no need for the sheriff, not at this point. But I'd like to take another look around. I'll go back there tomorrow and check it out."

Walt nodded. "I'll ride along with you."

Lacy moved farther into the room. "So will I." She'd love to see the expression on their faces if that man disappeared in front of them. And if he wasn't a ghost, well, she'd like to find out who he was and his reason for being here.

Both men stared up at her as if she were demented. "No, you won't," her father said. "You'll stay at home."

Lacy could have throttled him. "It would make more sense for me to come with you," she said in as reasonable a tone as she could manage. "I can show you exactly where it happened. Besides, I'm the one who saw the ghost. I should be part of the posse that tracks him down."

Walt folded his arms. "No. It's no place for a woman, Lacy."

"That's ridiculous! I've been there hundreds of times—and I've always been female."

Walt clenched his jaw. "It wasn't dangerous then."

"It isn't dangerous now! That ghost didn't hurt me. All he did was disappear."

"You were pretty shook up when I got there," Morgan put in.

Lacy turned on a heel to face him. "Of course I was shook up. I've never seen anyone vanish before. Now that I know it can happen, I won't be 'shook up' if it happens again." In truth, the idea of seeing that apparition disappear like smoke in front of her again was giving Lacy goose bumps. She wasn't going to let these men know that, though.

"No sense in taking that chance, is there?" Morgan grinned at her, his eyes a deep blue. "Not that I minded helping you deal with being 'shaken up.'"

Lacy gaped at him. Was he teasing her? Or was he…flirting with her?

Morgan lowered his voice to a soft, caressing

drawl. "And I'm not adverse to doing it again." He gazed into her eyes, his own warmer and bluer than Lacy had ever seen them before. He smiled briefly, averted his gaze and eased himself to his feet. "But it would be better all around if you stayed close to home." He swiped his hat off the table. "I'll drop by early tomorrow, Walt. We can ride out together from here."

Lacy recovered her senses. "But—"

No one paid any attention to her. Her father was standing next to Morgan, discussing arrangements with him. "Why don't you stable your horse here for the night and drive my truck home. You can bring it back in the morning and then we can head out."

"Appreciate it." Morgan murmured a polite good-night to Lacy and strode toward the door, accompanied by her father.

Lacy glared at both of them. They made a great pair—both chauvinists to their boot tips!

In spite of her annoyance, she still found herself appreciating the fit of Morgan's jeans around his muscled thighs.

It had to be that good-looking ghost. Seeing him must have done something to her libido.

2

"THIS IS REALLY, REALLY unfair," Lacy complained.

She pulled a bean out of the sink and gave it a vicious cut. The men had ridden off an hour ago to check on her ghost, leaving firm instructions that Lacy and Rita were to stay close to home until they returned.

Lacy was still feeling resentful. She didn't like being left behind and she also didn't like the fact that Morgan had looked just as appealing this morning as he had last night. Lacy was positive it was a temporary thing, caused by her daydreaming and that handsome ghost.

She remembered how he'd looked standing in front of those trees. She wouldn't mind seeing him again—but that wasn't on the schedule for now—grabbing another bean out of the sink was. "How come the macho men get to go look for the ghost while the women stay home and slice vegetables?"

Rita smiled patiently as she copied Lacy's motions. "You don't have to do this, you know."

"I might as well since I'm not allowed to do anything else!" That wasn't strictly true. She could always take a look at the tractor motor, clean the barn or check on the calves. Ignoring that, Lacy concentrated on being ticked off. "I have to 'stay close to home' until the men decide it's safe."

"Now, Lacy—"

"They even took rifles." Frowning, Lacy rested a hip against the kitchen counter. "What do you suppose they're going to do with those? Shoot my ghost?"

Rita patted her shoulder. "They aren't going to shoot anyone, honey."

"Good." Lacy turned back to the sink. "It wouldn't be any use if they did. Ghosts are already dead. It's the chief requirement for being a ghost."

Rita's brows drew together. "Do you really believe it was a ghost you saw?"

Lacy hesitated. "I...I'm not sure." Last night, she'd been so sure, but this morning, it seemed farfetched and impossible—almost like a dream. "It was getting dark. Maybe I just didn't see where that man went." She had seen where he'd gone, though. He'd vanished into thin air. She shuddered again as she recalled it. Live people didn't do things like that. It must have been her imagination or a trick of the weather—something explainable. "Besides, whose ghost could it have been? The only person who died around here was Grandpa and that ghost didn't look anything like him."

"I don't know." Her mother looked thoughtful for a moment. "There was that story about a rancher from around here getting shot by some gunslinger a long time ago. What was his name? Parkland...or Larkland...something like that."

"Oh, yeah." Lacy vaguely remembered hearing that story. "It could have been him, I suppose, although that man didn't look much like a rancher. He looked more like a gunslinger." She paused, her curiosity aroused by the story. "What happened to him anyway?"

"Who? The gunslinger? I have no idea. I don't even know if that's a true story. You could always ask your father. He knows more about these things than I do."

Lacy considered it, then shrugged it off. "It's not important. Besides, I probably did imagine the whole thing. There are no such things as ghosts—although that guy was almost too good-looking to be real."

Her mother's eyes opened wide with astonishment. "Good heavens, Lacy. I've never heard you say anything like that about a man."

Lacy flushed. "That's because I don't see a lot of good-looking ones around here."

Rita was still studying her curiously. "There are plenty of nice-looking men around here, honey."

Lacy couldn't name any. "Like who?"

"Let's see." Rita returned to working on the beans. "There's Bill Larentia. He's not a bad-looking man."

Lacy didn't consider Bill's bland features particularly appealing. "He's not a good-looking one, either. Besides, he's got the most outdated ideas about grazing that I've ever heard. It's a wonder his cattle don't starve to death."

Rita chuckled. "That has nothing to do with his looks." She thought for a moment. "How about Jon Taylor? He's got those big brown eyes—"

"Jon?" Lacy wrinkled her nose. "Jon looks like a hound, Mother! And he's got the worst taste in cattle in the county. You saw that last bull he bought! I don't think that animal could impregnate a goldfish much less a cow!"

Rita laughed again. "You do have a point." She was silent for a moment. Then her lips twitched. "What about Morgan Brillings? There's nothing wrong with his bulls."

The memory of Morgan's arms closing around her flashed unbidden across Lacy's mind. "No," she admitted. "He's got some of the best bulls in the county." Probably the best thighs in the county, too.

"And his grazing theories are very modern. Wasn't he one of the first in the county to take that course on holistic ranching?"

"Uh-huh." Morgan wasn't set in his ways like most of the men in the area. He was always willing to discuss new ideas.

Rita kept slicing vegetables. "I wouldn't call him gorgeous, but he is fairly good-looking."

"Mmmm." His features were strong but not un-attractive. The eyes were good. So were his arms and hands and... "Morgan's okay. But he's old enough to be my father!"

"He's only thirty-six, Lacy."

"Is he?" Lacy was almost twenty-eight, so he didn't have that many years on her. "He seems older. Besides, I'm not sure he'd know what to do with a woman if one fell into his lap."

"Lacy!"

"Well, I'm not. I've never seen him with any fe-male that didn't moo."

Rita laughed. "I guess I haven't, either—at least not recently, but—"

"That's probably because he's a confirmed bach-elor—which is a good thing because he'd drive a woman crazy." Lacy picked up her knife and returned to cutting up beans. "He's got the same outdated ideas about women as Dad does."

Rita patted her shoulder. "I'm afraid most of the men around here are a little like that. You just have to learn to deal with it. Otherwise you'll never get married."

"Good," Lacy muttered under her breath.

"Lacy!"

"I don't want to get married, Mom." She just wanted to have a romance with a handsome stranger. She thought about her ghost again. He couldn't be a ghost, but even if he was, he was out of the question. An affair with a ghost was too much on the kinky side for her. "We've had this discussion before. I'm not interested in marriage. I just want to stay here and run this ranch. I don't need a man around to do that."

"But—"

"It's hard enough with Dad. He's great and I love him, but he just won't let me do things my way. I grew up on this place. I spent three years studying agriculture, and I've been doing most of the work around here since his heart attack. But he still insists on telling me what to do and how to do it! Sometimes it's a little hard to take."

Rita was instantly sympathetic. "I know it is, honey. But he means well. And he likes to feel that he's helping."

Lacy felt ungrateful and bitchy for complaining. "I understand that. He's great and I've learned a lot from him. It's just that I'd like to do things my way."

One day she was going to do that, too. One day she'd be the person in charge. She could buy the cattle she wanted to buy, try some of the new techniques she'd been reading about—maybe even attempt breeding a few of the more exotic types. Of course when that happened, it would mean that her parents weren't here, and she didn't like that idea, either.

She flashed a conciliatory smile. "I'm not trying to boot you off the place, Mom. I can cope with Dad."

"You might not have to cope much longer," Rita murmured under her breath.

Lacy glanced over to see a worried frown crease Rita's brow. "What?"

"I just, um, think it might be time we moved." Rita picked up a towel and wiped her hands, taking great care to avoid meeting Lacy's eyes. "I want to live in town, Lacy. Your father does too much when he's on the ranch."

"I know. I try to—"

"You do everything you can. He's just like that. But if we lived in town, I think he'd take it easier." Rita bit her bottom lip. "Besides, most of our friends have moved into town. And I'd like your father to be closer to the doctor. If something happened out here…"

Lacy put her arm around her mother. "Nothing is going to happen, Mom." Her heart sank at the idea of her parents moving. She'd known that someday that would happen, but that someday had always been far in the future. She might be eager to run the place herself, but she couldn't imagine living in this house without them. She took one look at her mother's worried face and bit on her lip. She shouldn't be so selfish about this. "But if that's what you want to do, you should do it."

Rita's gaze met hers. "And what about you?"

Lacy returned to slicing beans. "Don't worry about me. I'll be fine."

Rita looked horrified. "We can't leave you here all by yourself!"

Lacy felt a little uneasy about it, too. "I'll be okay, really. Besides, that's always been the plan."

"No, it hasn't. The plan was that you would hire someone to help you. We were going to put a trailer in the yard and—"

"Then we'll do that," Lacy said.

"We can't." Rita sank into a chair. "We can't afford it now, Lacy."

That was a good point. Lacy winced. "I'll work something out."

Rita shook her head. "I don't think you can. Honey, sooner or later we have to face the fact that we aren't making a whole lot of money anymore. These past couple of years..."

Lacy didn't like thinking about that. "I know it's been bad, but—"

"It's been very bad." Rita took a deep breath. "And we're going to need some income to live in town. The only way we can do it is if we sell this place."

Lacy nodded. That's how it usually worked. The parents sold the land to their children—at a reduced rate, paid off over time, with a little help from the bank. "I'll talk to the bank. I can—"

"You can't, Lacy. There's no way you can pay a mortgage, clear all our debts and still have enough left over to support yourself and a hired man."

Another good point. "Well, uh..."

Rita's lips tightened. "Your father and I discussed

this last night. We think it's time we made some hard decisions."

Lacy's entire body went cold. "What sort of decisions?"

"To move." Rita raised her head and looked up into Lacy's eyes. "All of us."

"All of us?" Lacy repeated. "What do you mean, all of us?"

"I mean all of us. We're thinking of selling the ranch, Lacy."

Lacy gaped at her. "You can't be serious."

Rita looked unhappier than Lacy had ever seen her. "I don't think we have much choice."

"Of course you have a choice! I can take it over."

"You can't, honey. Not with the way our finances are now."

This couldn't be happening! "I'll work something out," Lacy said between gritted teeth. "I have to, Mom. I've lived here all my life! I pretty much run the place—with Dad's help, of course, but still, I do most of the work. You can't just sell it to someone else."

Rita winced. "I know you've worked hard, Lacy. And if things were different…if our financial situation was better or you were married…"

"Married?" Lacy glared at her. "What does my being married have to do with anything?"

"If you were married, there would be someone else here. You wouldn't be by yourself."

"I don't need anyone else!"

"You shouldn't be running the place on your own, dear. It's too big a job. Your father and I have been very selfish. We wanted to stay here after his heart attack and, well, we leaned on you more than we should. You work too hard, Lacy."

"I don't mind!"

"You should mind. You haven't had a chance to experience life...to meet someone—"

"I don't want to meet anyone."

"You should." Rita took a steadying breath. "You could move into town with us. You wouldn't have to work so hard. Mr. Krenshaw at the bank is always looking for people."

"The bank!" Lacy shuddered at the thought. "I couldn't work in the bank!"

"Or you could move to the city. Broaden your horizons. See something else of life. Maybe you'd meet someone there who—"

"I don't want to meet anyone, my horizons are broad enough, and I don't want to move anywhere else. I want to stay here and run this place."

"I know you do." Rita's shoulders drooped. "But I'm not sure that's an option."

"ONE HORSE, ONE RIDER," Walt concluded. He peered at the faint but unmistakable tracks in the dirt, then eased himself to a standing position. "Unless ghosts leave tracks, I'd say Lacy didn't see one."

Morgan stared at the evidence himself. Walt was right. The tracks clearly indicated that someone—a human someone—had been in the area. "That's how it looks," he agreed.

He took a long look at their surroundings. They were a good two hundred yards from the place where Lacy had insisted she'd seen her ghost. There hadn't been any tracks there, but that was explainable. That area was too rocky for many tracks to be left. And there weren't any tracks leading into the grove of trees, either. However, the ground there was covered with leaves and twigs. It was quite possible for someone to pass through them without leaving a sign.

"Looks like the fellow headed into the ravine," Walt concluded. He gestured toward the densely wooded area. "We could try tracking him down."

If he'd been alone, that was exactly what Morgan would do. However, he wasn't about to take any chances with Walt around. Rustlers were an unpredictable lot and Lacy had mentioned this one had been armed. "Not much point in that," Morgan decided. "The fellow is probably long gone by now."

Walt gave him a suspicious look, then shrugged. "I suppose you're right," he admitted with obvious reluctance.

Morgan rubbed the back of his neck as he considered the tracks again. "I just don't understand how he could have taken off without my spotting him— or hearing him. And I was over this patch of ground last night. How could I have missed this?"

Walt gave him a friendly slap on the back. "Don't blame yourself, Morgan. It was getting dark. Besides, you had Lacy to think about."

"Uh-huh." Still, Morgan felt uncomfortable about the situation, as if he was missing something. "Lacy's not going to be too happy about this," he commented as they went back to their horses. "She was so positive she saw a ghost."

"Lacy isn't happy about anything this morning," Walt grumbled, gathering the reins in his hand. "I don't know what's gotten into her. Last night she was seeing ghosts. This morning she was all put out because she couldn't ride along with us." He swung into the saddle. "She should know better than that. She's a woman! Women shouldn't be riding out after rustlers. And a ghost, for chrissake! She knows they don't exist."

Morgan grunted his agreement. Lacy's behavior had him puzzled, too. Most times she was such a sensible woman. On the other hand, maybe her being a woman did explain everything. "It's got to be those hormones," he concluded. "I guess they act up even in a person like Lacy."

"They were sure acting up this morning. She was mad as a hornet and she didn't care who knew it." Walt chuckled. "Too bad you weren't around. You handled her pretty good last night."

Morgan grinned at the memory. "It's just something Wade mentioned. If a woman gets all riled up, say something nice to her. It puts them off their stride." He never would have thought that technique would work with Lacy. Apparently, Wade had learned more about women than Morgan had given him credit for.

He'd also discovered that watching the flush in her cheeks and the sparkle in her eyes put him off his stride. He hadn't expected that to happen with Lacy, either.

"I wouldn't have expected that to work with Lacy," Walt remarked, echoing Morgan's own thoughts. "She's never shown much interest in men before."

"That so?" Did Lacy's reaction mean she was interested in him? No, it was just a woman thing—like hormones and clothes.

"It's a darn shame." Walt sighed again. "Her

mother and I would like to see her married, but that hasn't happened. And it doesn't look as if it's going to, either."

Morgan remained silent. He hadn't given Lacy's marital status much thought. Come to think of it, he couldn't recall seeing her with a man—at least not in any romantic capacity. She often stopped by the local bar to have a drink with the crowd, but that was just to shoot the breeze. She might have a dance or two with someone, but it wasn't always the same person. Most of the time, Morgan regarded her as just another rancher and forgot she was a woman.

"It's too bad," Walt rambled on. "Make things a lot easier if she was settled down. Maybe once she's off the ranch—"

"Off the ranch?" Surprised, Morgan glanced over at Walt. "You're not thinking of selling out, are you?"

"I don't have much choice." Walt cleared his throat. "Things haven't been going that well for us lately."

"You've had a couple of bad years," Morgan agreed. "That's bound to change, though."

"I can't wait, Morgan."

Morgan took another look at Walt. The other man was staring straight ahead, his jaw set. Morgan took a breath. "Look, if it's a question of money, I've got some put aside. I'd be more than happy to—"

Walt shook his head. "Nope. I don't borrow money from friends."

"Friends help—"

"I know, Morgan, and I appreciate the offer. But it's not just the money. I'm getting old. I'm over sixty, and my health isn't the best. And there's Rita to consider. She'd like to move into town. Most of her friends are there now." His tone warmed. "Plus, she'd like me to be closer to the doctor. It's not necessary, of course, but, well, you know women. They're always worrying."

Morgan nodded. His brother had mentioned the same thing a few times—and in the same indulgent tone, almost as if he was bragging. Morgan half envied them for having someone around who cared enough to worry.

"So it looks as if I'm going to have to sell," Walt continued. "I can't live in town without some income. If I had a son, well, he'd probably buy me out. But I don't have a son. I've got Lacy."

"She does a good job of running the place," Morgan added.

"I'm not disagreeing with that. But she can't stay on the place by herself. Besides, she should have a chance to meet other people, do other things. Find herself a husband."

Morgan pictured Lacy with some man in tow. Something about the picture didn't set well with him. "What does Lacy think of that?"

"Lacy doesn't seem interested in settling down with a man. I know she wants to run the place herself—and if circumstances were different, I wouldn't have any problem with that. She could hire some help and do a fine job of it. But she's not going to be in a position to hire anyone. And I sure as hell don't like the idea of leaving her there all alone." He gestured in the direction of the outcropping of trees. "Look what almost happened out here yesterday. A lone woman is vulnerable."

Morgan nodded. Walt was right. A woman

shouldn't live on an isolated ranch all by herself. Anything could happen. Still, he couldn't imagine Lacy being happy doing anything else. "You got any buyers in mind, or...?"

"Cal Robinson mentioned a couple of times that he wouldn't mind buying the place if I was of a mind to sell." Walt pulled his horse to a halt in the exact spot Lacy's animals had been standing last night. "I might have to take him up on it."

Morgan grimaced. Cal was a fine enough fellow, but he wasn't like the Johnsons. Morgan couldn't imagine himself dropping in on Cal the way he did Walt, Rita and Lacy. But he could understand Walt's position. He should be living in town, a lot closer to a doctor. And Lacy shouldn't be running the ranch single-handedly.

"THAT'S RIGHT," Morgan said into the phone. "Southwest corner of the Johnson ranch. We didn't see anyone, but the tracks were there." His gaze met Lacy's across her parents' kitchen. "Lacy got a look at him, but... Yeah, okay. Thanks, Dwight. I'll pass that on."

He hung up the phone, then wandered over to a chair and sat down. "The sheriff is going to check into it and he wants you to go in and give them a description, Lacy."

"All right." Lacy slumped in the kitchen chair, aware of a tremendous disappointment. Her ghost wasn't a ghost after all. It was a man. That wouldn't be too bad, except that this man probably wasn't one of the good guys. A good guy wouldn't be skulking around someone's property, doing a disappearing act when he was spotted.

She eyed Rita who was sitting in another chair, her eyes wide with concern. Walt was beside her, his hand on her arm, his face looking more worn than usual. Lacy didn't blame them. Cattle rustlers weren't the sort you wanted to have moving into the neighborhood. Not only were they not nice folks, but they could also put a large dent in the family income. Her stomach churned. The last thing this family needed was another dent in their income.

Morgan wrapped his hands around the coffee mug in front of him. "Dwight's going to warn everyone to keep up their guard. And he's getting more information from the folks up in Billings. In the meantime, he suggests we keep close to home or ride out in pairs."

"I really don't think that's necessary," Lacy objected. "The man I saw wasn't dangerous. He didn't even look like a cattle rustler. And he didn't hurt me!"

Morgan narrowed his eyes. "Still be wise for you to stick close to home, Lacy. A lone woman is an easy target."

"I'm no more of a target than anyone else," Lacy said, bristling at that. She frowned as Morgan and Walt exchanged a look, then banged her cup down onto the table. "Must you two look at each other every time I say something?"

"We don't have to, no," Morgan drawled. He smiled across the table at her. "As a matter of fact, I'd rather be looking at you."

Lacy's brain screeched to a halt, her body temperature rose to a dangerous high, and she sat in stunned silence while her mother went into a

"Won't you stay for dinner?" routine, which Morgan refused.

"I've got some chores around my place that need doing. Appreciate the offer, though." When she came to, he was shaking hands with her father and striding out the door.

Lacy blinked for a moment, then stormed to her feet. It was time she put a stop to this once and for all. She tore out the door after him.

Morgan had his foot in the stirrup when she caught up with him. "Just a minute, Morgan," Lacy said urgently. "I want to talk to you."

He glanced over his shoulder at her, then put his foot back on the ground and turned to face her. "Sure, Lacy. What's on your mind?"

"Everything!" She practically yelled as she placed her hands on her hips. "What *exactly* is going on here?"

"Going on?"

"You know what I mean. You've been…making comments ever since yesterday."

Morgan gave her an innocent look as if he had no idea what she was talking about. "Comments?"

"Personal comments. About me." He still looked puzzled. "And about the way I look," Lacy added.

"Oh," he said nonchalantly, his blue eyes glittering at her. "Well, you're a fine-looking woman, Lacy. Hard for a man not to notice."

It was a good line, but Lacy wasn't swallowing it. Until recently, she doubted Morgan had even realized she was a woman, much less a "fine-looking" one. He was just saying that to throw her off balance. "You've never noticed before."

Morgan's gaze flickered down her body and back up. "Guess I'm just making up for lost time."

He was doing it again! Lacy wasn't sure what was more infuriating—his actions, or her instant and unwelcome response. "Don't," she advised. "And while you're at it, I also want you to stop encouraging my father."

He raised an eyebrow. "How's that?"

"All this 'A woman alone is vulnerable' nonsense. My parents don't need to hear that. Dad is already making noises about selling this place rather than leaving me here to run it. He doesn't need any encouragement from you."

Morgan compressed his lips. "Walt does have a point. You shouldn't be here all on your lonesome."

"Why not? I've been pretty much running this place ever since Dad had that heart attack. I'm quite capable of doing it."

Morgan held up a hand. "Sure you are. But I don't think a ranch is any place for a single woman, and if you want me to say different, well, I can't go along with that."

"I don't want you to say anything! Just stay out of it. You're not helping the situation one little bit."

"Now look here, Lacy—"

"No, you look here. This is no joking matter. I could lose this place!" She glanced around the yard, swallowing back a lump in her throat. "How would you feel if you lost your ranch?"

Morgan winced. "I wouldn't like it at all, but—"

"This ranch means as much to me as your place does to you. I want it. I've spent all my life working to have it. I don't deserve to lose everything just because I'm female! It's not something I can do anything about, you know."

"It would be a darn shame if you could," Morgan drawled.

Lacy could have smacked him. She clenched her teeth in rage, fighting the urge to throw herself against him and pound her fists against his broad chest. "Stuff it in your boot!" she snarled.

Startled, Morgan took a backward step. "Now, Lacy—"

"And you can stuff your stupid chauvinistic opinions there, as well! If you were any sort of a friend, you'd be trying to help instead of trying to get me out of here!"

Morgan's lips thinned. "Hold on there. I'm not trying to—"

"This is *my* ranch!" Lacy ranted. "I'm not going to lose it because *you* don't think I should have it!"

Turning, she stomped into the house. Men! She wished more of them would turn into ghosts!

3

IF GETTING MARRIED DID to her what it had done to Janice Delany, Lacy wanted no part of it.

She sat in an elegant gray-and-black chair in Janice's perfectly organized kitchen, watching her redheaded friend bustle around. In the bygone pre-Oliver days, Janice had been a normal human being. She'd helped out at the family ranch, she'd been one heck of a barrel racer, and she'd been as interested in cattle and horses as Lacy.

All that had changed after she married Oliver. Now Janice's conversation revolved around Oliver—what Oliver thought, what Oliver said, and how she was going to get Oliver's socks clean. Most of the time, that drove Lacy around the bend. However, Janice had always been a good friend, and this morning, Lacy felt as if she really needed one.

"Try one of these," Janice invited as she set a plate of freshly baked cookies on the table. "I'm not too sure about them, though. I'm afraid they might be a bit overdone."

Lacy chose a cookie and took a bite. They were oatmeal raisin, of course. Oliver loved oatmeal raisin cookies. "They're fine, Jan."

"You sure they aren't too crispy?"

Lacy took another bite. "They're just right. Honest."

"Good." Janice looked relieved. "Oliver likes them more on the chewy side, you know."

"Does he?" Lacy added this piece of trivia to the growing list of things she'd never thought she'd know about Janice's husband.

Janice filled her coffee cup, apparently happy now that her cookies had passed inspection, and returned to their original conversation. "I wouldn't worry too much about that rustler, Lacy. Oliver says he's probably long gone by now."

"It's not the rustler," Lacy confessed, propping her chin on her hand. "It's everything. We're broke. Dad's seriously talking about selling the place. Besides all that, everyone is on a 'Lacy shouldn't be on the ranch alone' kick—including Morgan."

"Morgan?" Janice took another pan of cookies out of the oven. "Did Morgan say that in his sexy drawl?"

"What?"

"Morgan," Janice explained. "I just love the way he talks." She lowered her voice to mimic Morgan's tone. "You shouldn't be all by your lonesome, Lacy honey. Is that what he said?"

Lacy got prickles up her back just from thinking about Morgan's voice. "Sort of, I guess, but—"

"I wish he'd say that to me. I'd agree with him." Janice batted her eyelashes. "You're right, Morgan baby. How about coming in and keeping me company. Of course, you'll have to dispose of my husband first."

"Janice!"

Janice's small, round face lit up with amusement. "I'm just trying to cheer you up. I'm not serious. I'd never cheat on Oliver." She paused. "But if I was going to, I'd do it with Morgan. There's something about the strong, silent type, isn't there? Besides, you've got to admit he's put together real well. Those muscular arms...not to mention muscular thighs...mmm."

Lacy hadn't thought much about his arms, but she'd certainly noticed his thighs. They were great all right. She scowled at the thought. She didn't want to think about Morgan's thighs. "I wish he'd be silent about this," she grumbled.

"Oh, Lacy." Janice sat down across from her and reached over and squeezed her right arm. "Morgan is just being a man. It's all that testosterone. It goes straight to their heads and replaces all the brain tissue. It even happens to Oliver sometimes."

"It does?" Lacy asked, astonished. She'd often thought that about Oliver, but she'd never heard Janice voice even one disparaging word about the man.

"Uh-huh. But in this case, I don't see it as bad advice. If there are rustlers around..."

"He sure didn't look like a rustler." Lacy took a breath. "As a matter of fact, when I first saw him, I thought he was a ghost."

"A ghost?" Janice's warm hazel eyes sparkled with curiosity. "Really? Tell me all about it."

Lacy briefly described her encounter. "And then it was as if he...disappeared into thin air," she concluded. "I don't know what happened. It was getting dark. And I had been out all day. Maybe I did have too much sun. Or something."

"Or maybe you really saw a ghost," Janice said, nodding.

Lacy stared at her. She hadn't expected Janice to

believe her any more than anyone else. "It wasn't. I told you. The men found tracks."

Janice made a face. "That doesn't mean anything. Men always find what they want to find. They go to a place called Rustler's Ravine and they expect to find a rustler. It never occurs to them that a rustler with one ounce of common sense wouldn't hang out in a place called that! They're more likely to be in Good Guy Gulch." She raised an eyebrow. "Besides, where is it written that ghosts don't leave tracks?"

Lacy shrugged. "I don't know. I don't know anything about ghosts. But I assume—"

"Well, I do," Janice boasted comfortably. "I've seen tons of episodes of *Paranormal Hot Line*. It's on Tuesday nights at ten. Oliver even watches it with me sometimes—but don't tell him I told you that!"

Lacy blinked. "You and Oliver watch *Paranormal Hot Line?*"

"Us and millions of other people." Janice didn't seem the least bit embarrassed to admit this. "You would not believe the number of ghost sightings there are in this country."

Was she serious? Lacy gazed into her friend's earnest face and decided she was. What happened to women when they got married? Janice used to be so rational. Then she'd gotten married. Now she baked cookies and watched *Paranormal Hot Line*.

"One thing's very clear, Lacy." Janice wiped her hands on a green-and-white-checked towel. "Ghosts do not show up without a good reason. It takes a lot of psychic energy for them to cross over from the other dimension."

"Does it?" Seeing a ghost was one thing. Having this conversation with Janice about it was something else. It could have something to do with Oliver, Lacy speculated. Perhaps there was an odd streak running through him.

"Uh-huh." Janice nodded decisively. "So it seems to me that if your ghost went to all the effort of making an appearance, you should put a little effort into finding out why he came here."

"Right." In spite of her skepticism, Lacy was intrigued. "And how would I go about doing that?"

"Well…" Janice tapped her fingers on the tabletop while she considered her answer. "The first step would be to find out who he is—or was, I mean."

"I don't know…"

"It shouldn't be that difficult to figure out. He was on your land. That means he had to be there sometime during his life. Ghosts only go to places they've been to during their lifetime. It's something to do with their cosmic connections to the reality of the universe."

"That's, uh, fascinating, Janice, but—"

Janice snapped her fingers and bounced to her feet. "I know. That book about the history of the area that old Mrs. Kilpatrick put together a few years ago. Maybe we can find him in there."

Before Lacy could stop her, she'd dashed into the living room. Lacy stayed where she was, stunned by this turn of events. Fresh air. That's what her friend needed. More fresh air and a lot less Oliver.

Janice bustled back into the room, clutching a fat black book. "Here it is." She spread it out on the kitchen table in front of them. "Maybe we can find him in here."

"I don't know, Janice. I—"

"It can't hurt to take a look." Janice started turning pages. "How old do you think he was?"

Lacy started to object, then gave in. There was no stopping Janice when she'd made up her mind. Besides, there was a faint chance that maybe Janice was onto something. "He wasn't old. He was closer to our age—in his mid-thirties, I'd say."

"Mid-thirties, hmmm. Let's see...." Together they flipped through the pages, peering at the faded photographs. "Here are the Taylors." Janice pointed to one picture of twelve unsmiling individuals. "They all look a little like hound dogs, don't they? Here's Howie Troshak's family...Josh Turnbull..."

"You know, Mom did mention something about a rancher who was shot around here a long time ago," Lacy mused. "Parksomething or Larksomething."

Janice turned another page. "How about Larkspur?" She tapped her fingernail against a photograph of an elderly man, standing with a much younger dark-haired woman. "This is them." She read from the text. "'Frank Larkspur and his daughter, Sarah. Sarah took over the Larkspur ranch after her father passed away.'" She shook her head. "It couldn't have been him. It says here he died in some sort of mining accident." Janice turned a page. "Your mother must have been thinking about Karl Robinson. According to the book, he was shot by some gunslinger. Here's his picture."

Lacy studied it eagerly, but the heavyset man in no way resembled her ghost. "That's not him." She sighed.

"He has to be in here somewhere," Janice insisted. She turned another page. "Too bad he wasn't this guy. He's cute."

Lacy had pretty much concluded by now that this was a waste of time. She glanced at the old photo almost with disinterest, then froze. "Who...uh...who is he?"

"The gunslinger who shot Karl." Janice furrowed her brow as she read. "His name was Jake Malone." She looked up at Lacy. "What's wrong?"

"It's him." Lacy ran her finger over the faded photograph. "That's the man I saw. Jake Malone. The gunslinger."

YOU'RE NOT HELPING the situation one little bit!

Morgan gave the yearling a final pat, shoved his hands into his pockets and stomped across the yard and on into his house. Darn Lacy anyway. Ever since their little scene outside the Johnsons' house yesterday, he'd been replaying her words over and over in his mind. And every time he did, he felt bad—not because he'd stuck to his guns about her running the ranch by herself. He was right about that. Still, he felt bad. He felt bad for the Johnsons, he felt bad for Lacy, and most of all, he felt bad because she was right. He wasn't doing anything to help the situation.

He wandered into his living room, threw himself down in a chair and stacked his boots on the footstool that matched the chair he was sitting in. All the furniture used to be a dull brown color. Now there were two deep green chairs and a rust-colored sofa. The cushions on the sofa were a combination of the dark green and rust. He had Wade's wife to thank for this. It had taken a little time to get used to the change, but now Morgan liked it.

Morgan rested his head back and closed his eyes.

Walt and Rita had been darn good neighbors for a number of years. Morgan had been in his early twenties when his father passed away. By then, Wade had been heavily involved with the navy, leaving Morgan to take over the ranch alone. Walt had always been there for him, offering advice when Morgan needed it, providing encouragement and support. And Rita—well, Rita was like the mother he'd never had. She'd cooked him countless meals, made sure he wasn't alone for Christmas and other holidays…and when he'd broken his ankle a few years back, it was Rita who'd stopped by every day to make sure he was all right. He hated like hell to see them sell their ranch. And he hated even more to think of Lacy losing it. She was right. She'd worked darn hard to keep the place going. She didn't deserve to lose it just because she was a woman.

But he couldn't think of anything to do about it. Walt refused to accept a loan and Morgan couldn't fault him for that. It was too bad Lacy hadn't had the sense to get married years ago. Then she'd have had a man to help her and she wouldn't be in this situation. Why hadn't she done that? She was a fine-looking woman—and a sensible one, too. At least she had been before this ghost nonsense.

If it was nonsense. He pictured her as she'd come flying out of the trees toward him. She'd sure been scared of something. His lips curled upward as he thought of her throwing herself into his arms. Damn but she'd felt good pressed up against him like that, with her breasts pushing against his chest. She wasn't a big woman, but she was well developed. Made a man wonder how she'd look when she was stark naked. A good guess as to how she'd appear flashed across his brain. Morgan enjoyed it for a second, then realized what he was doing and straightened. What the hell was the matter with him? He'd known Lacy all his life and he'd never concerned himself with how she'd look naked before! Why was he doing it now?

It was probably because he was alone so much. He hadn't minded it before, but now, well, now he was getting tired of living by himself. He'd enjoy having someone to come home to…someone to share his day with…and someone to share his nights with, as well. Wade was lucky he'd found a wife. Maybe he should, too. It was well past time he did if he was hoping to have kids. If he didn't, what was going to happen to his ranch when he became too old to run it? He didn't have any heirs. Wade and Cassie were talking about having children, but even if they did, Morgan couldn't see any child of Wade's being content to take over the ranch. Most likely they'd take after Wade, join up with some fighting group and spend their time either traveling or getting shot at. Besides, a kid should be born and raised on a ranch before he took it over. It would be best all around if Morgan married and had his own children. He shoved the idea aside. He didn't have time to find a wife right now…and he wasn't sure he knew how to go about doing it.

Sighing, he started to rise, then dropped back into the chair again. What was the matter with him? There was a perfectly good woman practically next door…a woman who needed a husband so she could keep her ranch.

Lacy!

He turned the idea around in his mind. Why

didn't he marry Lacy? She was a levelheaded sort—with the exception of this ghost thing, that is. She'd be handy around the ranch, he liked talking to her, and she probably wouldn't go around redecorating everything. She had good, strong ranching genes that, along with his, would produce a fine passel of children all born and bred to be ranchers. And from the way she felt against him, well, he'd say creating those kids wouldn't be much of a hardship, either.

Marriage to her would be perfect. Walt and Rita could move into town and not have to worry about Lacy. Morgan could buy them out without their having to accept a loan. He and Lacy could amalgamate their properties. Lacy could keep running the Johnson place if that's what she wanted. She wouldn't have to work so hard. Morgan would have a wife and he wouldn't have to spend a lot of time looking for one. Hell, they'd even have a second home for the kids when they grew up.

It was starting to sound like a darn good idea that tied up a lot of loose ends.

MORGAN'S PICKUP was parked in front of her parents' house when Lacy arrived home.

Lacy made a face at it. "Terrific," she muttered as she parked her own truck. "I suppose he's telling my parents more malarkey about how a woman has no business running a ranch." He better not be. If he was, she just might flatten his tires!

Lacy giggled at the notion, still light-headed and stunned after making her amazing discovery. She had seen a ghost after all. The ghost of a gunslinger. She even had a name. Jake Malone!

She climbed out of the truck. Now they could for-

get about this "Lacy has to stay close to home" nonsense and she could get back to the business of
ranching.

That was, if anyone believed her.

Lacy closed the truck door and headed toward the
house. That was unlikely to happen. Her father
hadn't believed she'd seen a ghost in the first place.
He wasn't going to suddenly accept that it was the
ghost of some old gunslinger. The sheriff wouldn't
believe it and Morgan certainly wouldn't believe it.
He and her father would probably just sit there and
look at each other. Then they'd use this as another
damning piece of evidence that women were inca-
pable of running ranches. "Those women," they'd
say. "They can't be left alone for one minute or they
start seeing ghosts in books. It's got to be those hormones."

She chuckled at the thought, then sobered. That
might not be too far off what the men would say. It
might be better if she didn't mention this to them.
She was too excited not to tell someone about it.
She'd spill the whole tale to her mother. Rita might
not believe it, either, but she'd be more understanding than the men.

She opened the green-and-white outer door and
stepped into the back entranceway. "Hello?" she
called out. "Mom! Dad! Where is everybody?"

It was her mother who answered. "We're in the
living room, Lacy."

There was an unusual tone in her voice—not excitement exactly. Almost wariness. Lacy's lips tightened as she identified it. Now what had happened?
Had the sheriff found a rustler out there after all?

Maybe that's why her gunslinger had appeared—to warn her of danger.

She hurried through the kitchen into the living room and stopped at the doorway. Her parents were sitting together on the sofa, with Morgan in his usual chair at right angles to them. He rose to his feet as she entered the room. "Hello, Lacy."

"Hi." His shoulders looked very broad encased in a black-and-gray-striped Western shirt with snapped-down pockets and shiny silver buttons. Lacy caught her breath. He was wearing a pair of black jeans along with the shirt and had rolled the sleeves up to his elbows. The dark outfit emphasized the breadth of his chest and along with his equally black hair and tanned skin made him look more masculine than ever. Her gaze traveled down his shoulders, pausing at his forearms. Janice was right. He did have great muscles.

She compressed her lips as she realized what she was doing and gave him a cool smile. "Hi, Morgan."

She glanced over at her parents and felt a prickle of unease. Her father's cheeks were flushed, his gray eyes sparkling as if he was pleased about something. Her mother seemed a lot less pleased. She sat beside her husband, her forehead furrowed, her lips pressed together in a familiar expression—one she used when she was biting her tongue. Lacy's uneasiness increased, not just because of the look on her mother's face, either. There was an air of expectancy in the room, as if all the occupants were waiting for something to happen. They couldn't have heard about her ghost yet. Something else was going on—something that concerned her.

Walt confirmed her suspicions. "It's a good thing

you're here," he said heartily. "We wanted to talk to you."

"You did?" Lacy looked from one to the other, searching for clues. "About what?"

"The ranch," Walt started. "You see—"

Rita put a hand on his arm. "Walt, I'm not sure now is the time—"

"It's as good a time as any, Rita. After all, this does concern her." He gestured toward a chair. "Don't just stand there, Lacy. Come on in and sit down."

Lacy moved reluctantly into the room and perched on the edge of a chair. Most of her attention was on her parents, but out of the corner of her eye she saw Morgan settle back down. Even as concerned as she was, part of her still noticed the way the denim stretched tautly across his legs. She forced herself to look away and focus on her father's face. "What about the ranch?"

"Well…" Walt cleared his throat. "Morgan and I have been discussing our problem."

"Oh?" Lacy blinked a few times.

"And Morgan here has come up with an interesting solution."

"Has he?" She tried not to look at Morgan but did anyway. The top few buttons on his shirt were unbuttoned, revealing curly chest hair a shade lighter than the strands falling across his forehead. She turned her attention back to her father. "What would that be?"

Walt chuckled. "I suppose you could call it sort of an amalgamation of properties."

"Amalgamation of properties?" Lacy's gaze traveled around the room while her brain did a quick memory search of the word *amalgamate*. "What's that? Some kind of…of new grazing theory?"

"Not exactly." Morgan cleared his throat. "I suggested we…join forces, so to speak."

"Join forces?"

"Uh-huh. And it should work out just fine. I figure I can handle both places without too many problems. I've got Eddie…and Matt Walburn has been helping me out from time to time. He'd probably be willing to do it on a more regular basis, and I can always hire more men if need be. There are a lot of details to work out, of course, but…"

He went on talking. Lacy listened with half her brain while the other half focused on the fact that he did have a sexy drawl. She tried not to think about it while she concentrated on what he was saying. If he was taking care of both places, what was she…?

Her body suddenly lost all its heat. "Just a minute," she interrupted. "What exactly is going on here? Surely you're not suggesting that *you* take over our ranch?"

Morgan looked at her as if she was a little slow. "In a manner of speaking, but—"

Every drop of blood in Lacy's body rushed to her feet, then back up to her head. "No," she whispered. Then louder, "*No!*"

"Now, Lacy…" Morgan started.

Lacy sprang to her feet, incensed. "This is your great solution? You buy us out? *You* get *my* ranch?"

Walt stirred. "It's not quite—"

"Dad, I can't believe you'd do this!" Lacy glowered at him. "I can't believe you'd discuss selling the place without talking to me!"

"I'm not exactly selling it, Lacy. Morgan would be—"

"Morgan!" Lacy practically spit out his name. "I suppose that makes it all right—because it's Morgan!" Her voice rose. "There's no difference between selling the ranch to Morgan and selling to someone else! In both cases, I lose it!"

"Lacy…"

Lacy gasped in a breath in a futile attempt to remain calm while all her dreams were crumpling in front of her. "How could you do this? How could you? I love this place. You know that."

"Of course I do. I—"

"It's all I've ever wanted—and I've worked hard to have it. It should be mine."

Walt started to look angry. "You know darn well that—"

"I'm willing to buy you out, too, you know. I can do it. I just need a little time! Or aren't I going to get that chance because I'm a woman? Because if it is—"

"Now you just hold on there, Lacy," Morgan interrupted in his now infuriating drawl. "I'm not talking about buying the place! I'm talking about marriage."

"Marriage?" For a second, Lacy couldn't figure out what that word meant, either. "Who's getting married?"

"No one's getting married yet," Morgan soothed. "But I'm suggesting that you and I—"

"You and I?" Her heart sank as his words permeated her brain. Was he suggesting that they…no, he couldn't be. She looked into his brilliant blue eyes and got the distinct impression that he was.

Morgan confirmed it. "That's right. I think you and I should get married."

Lacy sank limply back onto the chair and stared at her parents. Two days ago, she was leading a normal life. Then she'd seen a ghost. Today, she'd identified him as gunslinger, Jake Malone. And now, for no reason, out of the blue, with absolutely no warning, Morgan had decided they should get married.

Had the entire world gone crazy or was it just her little corner of it?

"I don't believe this," she muttered. She kept staring at her parents in blank dismay. "First Morgan comes up with this ridiculous idea that we should get married. Now you're telling me that you think I should do it!" She was still having problems taking that in. "Is this really happening or am I having a bad dream?"

Walt and Rita exchanged a concerned look before focusing on her. "We didn't say we thought you should do it," Rita said cautiously. "Your father just said he thought you should consider it."

She sat in astonished silence while Morgan and her father went on to discuss how this whole thing would work. Then, the next thing she knew, Morgan was telling her to give it serious consideration and walking out the door.

She turned to her father. "You don't really expect me to marry Morgan just so I can keep this ranch, do you?"

Walt opened his mouth and Rita spoke quickly. "No, of course not, darling. We aren't suggesting you do anything you don't want to do." She dug her elbow into her husband's side. "Are we, Walt?"

"Of course not," Walt growled.

"Good," said Lacy. "Because—"

"But there's no reason for you *not* to do it," Walt interrupted. "Morgan's a good man, Lacy."

He was also a darn attractive one, but that was beside the point. "The world is full of good men, Dad. You don't expect me to marry any of them, do you?"

Walt's eyebrows came down warningly and he lowered his tone, as well. "No, I do not! For one thing, there aren't a whole lot of them lining up *to* marry you!"

Lacy tightened her lips resentfully. "I know that! And it doesn't bother me, either. I've told you both that I do *not* want to get married!"

Walt's gusty sigh could have blown over one of the willows surrounding the house. "Well, you should! A single woman on a ranch isn't a good idea. You know that, Lacy! Look what happened the other day with that rustler. If Morgan hadn't come along—"

"He wasn't a rustler! He was a ghost! People don't normally rush off to get married just because they've seen one of them!"

Walt's expression grew thunderous. "Damn it, Lacy—"

"And even if I did want to get married, I'd want to do it for the same reason you two got married. Because you were in love!" She swung her head to look at her mother. She was a woman. She should understand. "That wasn't even mentioned! Morgan just sat there talking about amalgamating our properties!" Amalgamating their properties! Just thinking about that infuriated her. It wasn't that she wanted Morgan to be madly in love with her, but still… "I don't know why he came up with this harebrained idea in the first place! He's never shown any interest in getting married to me or anyone else before."

Rita nodded agreement. "I know he hasn't. But I think he's looking on it differently now that Wade's married. His wife is such a sweet little thing. And she did re-cover all of Morgan's furniture. It really perked up the place. That sort of thing can make a man view marriage in a different light."

"It can, can it?" Is that what Morgan wanted—a wife who would cook and clean and re-cover furniture? "Well, I can't sew. Do you think when Morgan finds that out, he'll withdraw his proposal?"

Walt scowled. "I don't—"

"I wouldn't even call it a proposal," Lacy interrupted. "It sounded more as if he was making an offer to buy one of our bulls. He spent more time discussing it with Dad than he did with me." Her indignation increased as she mentally replayed the conversation. He'd actually described it as joining forces. Joining forces! That wasn't the way any woman wanted to be invited into matrimony! Even the densest of men should know that. A woman wanted to be swept off her feet, hear declarations of undying love and irresistible passion, not a business proposition. Morgan hadn't said any of those things. If he had, she might have reacted differently. She wouldn't have said yes, but she wouldn't have felt so insulted, either.

Her anger with him, with her parents, with the entire situation, kept growing in magnitude.

"He just, uh, probably hasn't had much practice," Rita soothed. "I'm sure—"

"Well, he can practice on someone else!" Lacy

jumped to her feet. "I'm sorry, folks. I know it would solve a lot of problems for all of us, but I am *not* going to do it. I refuse to get married just because we're broke, Morgan's sister-in-law re-covered his furniture and I saw a ghost!"

4

WASN'T ANYONE GOING to say anything?

Lacy hid a yawn behind her fist, took another forkful of eggs and eyed her parents sitting at the breakfast table. Normally this was a busy, noisy meal, with her going over her plans for the day, her father arguing with her about them and her mother putting in her two cents' worth every now and then.

This morning, it was different. The only person talking was Lacy—and she was starting to suspect that she was the only person listening, as well. So far she'd mentioned moving the cattle from the east pasture, combining hay and rounding up the calves. Apart from a grunt or two, neither of her parents had made a single comment.

She also seemed to be the only person eating. Rita toyed with her breakfast, dangling her fork as if she'd forgotten it was there, then methodically pushing her eggs from one side of the plate to the other. Walt wasn't much better. He'd pushed aside his half-empty plate and was sitting back in his chair, his hands wrapped around a coffee cup while he peered inside as if trying to determine the contents.

Lacy looked from one to the other, then made another stab at normalcy. "I think I'd better take a look at the truck this afternoon. It's been running a little rough. It could be that the engine needs a complete overhaul."

She took a bite of her toast. That should get her father going. He'd given that truck a good going-over a couple of weeks ago. Under normal circumstances, her questioning his abilities would have caused an explosion. But this morning all he did was grunt. "Uh-huh."

"Whatever you think, dear," Rita murmured. She exchanged a look with her husband, then returned to playing with her food.

Lacy gave up. "What is the matter with you two this morning?" She pushed aside her plate and swiped a napkin across her mouth. "Every time I say anything, you look at each other. And you've hardly said a word. I've had better conversations with Oscar!"

They looked at each other again. "We're just a little distracted this morning," Rita said apologetically.

"That's right. We are." Walt set down his cup with a bang. "We're thinking about what Morgan suggested yesterday. You haven't said anything about that, Lacy. What are you planning on doing?"

Rita put a hand on his arm. "Now, Walt..."

Walt glowered from under his heavy eyebrows. "It's our lives, too, Rita. We've got a right to know what's going on."

"Nothing is going on!" Lacy retorted. She watched their faces swing her way. "I haven't said anything about Morgan this morning because there's nothing to say. I said it all yesterday. I'm not going to marry him and that's that."

There was dead silence, followed by the sound of

her father's chair legs scraping across the linoleum as he pushed back from the table and surged to his feet. "I think you're being a darn fool!" he growled. "There's no reason in the world for you not to marry Morgan. He's a good man and he'd take care of you. What more does a woman want?"

"How about romance?" Lacy shot back.

"Romance?" Walt gave a snort of disgust. "Since when did you give two hoots about romance?" He stalked out of the room, his back stiff with disapproval.

Lacy watched him leave, then turned to her mother. "You understand, don't you, Mom? I can't marry Morgan just because it would be convenient for us."

"I know, dear." Rita rose and began gathering the breakfast things off the table. "And I don't expect you to, either. I just think the matter deserves a little more thought."

"I have thought about it." Lacy picked up some plates and carried them over to the sink. That was for sure. She hadn't thought about much else all night. Even when she'd slept, Morgan's proposal had stuck to her brain like a burr on Oscar. Her dreams had been filled with half-formed images of them together...and some of those images had been darn close to erotic.

Just thinking about them brought heat to her cheeks and a rush to her pulse.

"I mean serious thought, Lacy. You and Morgan have been friends for a long time. You get along well together. You enjoy each other's company. You've got a lot in common. I've sometimes wondered if, well, if there isn't more between you two than either of you realizes."

Lacy set down the plates with a clatter. Where did her mother get these ideas? Granted, she did spend a lot of time with Morgan, but that didn't mean anything. It was difficult not to spend time with him. He was a frequent dinner guest, he attended the same functions she attended, and there was no one she liked discussing ranching methods with as much as him. However, that did *not* mean there was anything between them besides the casual friendship she had with all the other ranchers.

It certainly didn't mean she wanted to be Mrs. Morgan! "There isn't anything between us!"

Rita leaned back against the counter. "You don't have to make any decisions right away. Why don't you let this rest for a while. Spend a little time with Morgan. You never know—"

"I've seen Morgan at least twice a week ever since I can remember! Spending more time with him won't change anything."

Rita got a funny smile on her face. "You never know." She opened the dishwasher and started loading. "You never know."

"I do so know!"

Her mother just shrugged, and Lacy gave up. Her saying "I'm not going to marry him" didn't seem to sink in with these people. She needed to do something to put this issue to bed, so to speak. Then beds made her think naughty thoughts, which increased her annoyance. "As a matter of fact, I'm going to go over to Morgan's place right now and tell him no."

Rita looked up, alarmed. "I'm not sure that's a

good idea. If you'd give it a little more consideration—"

"I've considered it enough!" Lacy snatched the
truck key off the hook and made for the door.
Enough was enough. The only way to deal with this
was head-on. "It was nice of Morgan to offer to sacrifice himself to help us out, but it's not necessary,
and I'm going to tell him so. Then we can all stop
thinking about it and start looking for another solution."

"I think you're being too hasty."

"I don't!" Lacy pushed open the screen door, concentrating hard on not noticing the look of disappointment on her mother's face. It was understand-
able, she supposed. Morgan had come up with a
solution of sorts to their dilemma. It just wasn't a solution she could live with, that's all. Marrying Morgan? Really! What would these people think of next?

She drove to Morgan's place on automatic pilot,
her mind occupied by what she was going to say.
She'd never had a marriage proposal before—if his
suggestion of joining forces could be considered a
marriage proposal. She wasn't quite clear on the
proper protocol for turning one down. "There's no
way I'm going to marry you" seemed a little harsh.
She didn't want to hurt Morgan's feelings—not that
she thought he had any emotion tied up in the issue.
He was just trying to help them out. She toyed with
other approaches and finally settled on, "I've
thought it over, Morgan, and although it was kind of
you to offer it, I'm sure you agree that marriage is
out of the question."

She didn't expect Morgan to put up much of a fuss
about it. He didn't want to marry her any more than

she wanted to marry him. He would probably be relieved.

Although it was quite early, there were signs of activity at Morgan's well-kept place when she pulled into his yard. The barn door was wide open, and a flatbed truck, loaded down with hay, stood beside it. She could see Eddie Bowman, Morgan's hired man, shifting around bales of hay inside the barn. He stopped what he was doing to wave at her.

Lacy waved back and climbed out of the truck. It was easy to see that Morgan was doing a lot better than her family was. The barn and the other outbuildings had been freshly painted, the grass around the house was neatly mowed, and the flatbed truck was new. The place was a touch on the barren side, though. There were no flowers and shrubs to brighten the yard, and none of the cheerful lawn ornaments her mother set out to give their place a homey touch. Lacy had subconsciously noticed that a long time ago, but she had never given it much thought. Now, it struck her that even if she didn't know it, she'd have no problem guessing that there wasn't a female in residence here.

And there wasn't going to be one, either—at least not her. She wasn't the flower-planting type.

She started toward the barn as Eddie came out of it. "Hey, Lacy," he said. He wandered over to her, his round, friendly face alive with curiosity. "You're out and about early this morning."

"I suppose." Lacy took a long breath of cool morning air. "I wanted to talk to Morgan."

"Oh?" Eddie's curious expression increased and Lacy winced. She hoped Morgan hadn't mentioned his harebrained idea to Eddie. He was a great guy, but he and his wife were terrible gossips.

"Is he here?"

"Uh-huh." Eddie grinned and thrust a thumb toward the shed beside the barn. "He's over there, swearing at the tractor. Just listening to him go at it makes me darn grateful I'm not a piece of equipment."

"Thanks." Lacy lifted her chin and marched toward the shed. The sooner she got this matter settled the better, before Morgan—or her parents—could spread it around.

Her steps faltered as she rounded the corner of the barn. Morgan was halfway up the tractor, muttering to himself as he examined the engine. His position caused his denim jeans to stretch over his buttocks and thighs. Janice was right about him, Lacy decided as she stopped to appreciate the view. He was put together real fine.

That still didn't mean she wanted to take a trip to the altar with him. Lacy cleared her throat and ordered herself not to think about his thighs. "Morgan?"

He turned to look over his shoulder at her. "Well, hi there, Lacy." He slid to the ground. "I didn't hear you drive up. Guess I was too busy with this goldarn tractor here." He snatched a rag out of his back pocket and used it to wipe at the grime on his fingers. "You're out early this morning."

"I guess I am." Morgan had a streak of grease along one cheek, a matching spot on his nose and a few more on the faded green T-shirt that sported a Montana's Wild logo above a picture of a bucking horse. The T-shirt and the horse seemed to emphasize his rock-solid chest—a chest that had felt awfully good under her cheek.

Morgan's welcoming expression transformed to concern. "There isn't anything wrong, is there?"

I saw a ghost, you proposed, I might lose my ranch, my parents are acting like they live in a silent movie, and I've developed a thigh fixation. "Not really, no. I just, uh, wanted to talk to you." She spotted Eddie out of the corner of her eye. He was standing just outside the barn, watching them with interest. "Alone," she added.

"Oh?" Morgan squinted at her as if he had no idea why she might want to do that, then gestured toward the house. "How about if we head inside, then? I've got some coffee on."

"That would be great." Coffee. Ordinary, normal coffee. That's what she needed—that and some cold water to splash on her overheated body.

Morgan opened the door and motioned her inside. "You just help yourself to coffee," he invited as the door closed behind them. "I'll take a stab at getting some of this grease off me."

He kicked off his boots and headed down the hall. Lacy watched him go, then removed her own boots and started toward the kitchen. The Brillings house was bigger than the three-bedroom bungalow she shared with her parents. It was a two-story structure, with a living room, kitchen and dining room on the main floor, as well as a bathroom and a room off the kitchen Morgan used as an office. All the rooms had been freshly painted in a creamy white. Lacy chuckled as she recalled how Morgan had complained about his sister-in-law's forcing him to do that.

She stopped when she reached the living room and stood in the doorway, looking around. She'd been here countless times, but this was the first time she'd seen the room since the furniture had been recovered. Her mother was right, she decided. The room did look better with green-and-rust-colored furniture than it had when everything was a dull brown. Like the outside, though, it showed the absence of a female presence. There were no knickknacks on the single bookshelf, only books. The end tables held only functional-looking lamps. There were no ornaments or lacey doilies that her mother liked to spread around—and no vases of dried flowers, either. The room was very clean and somehow very empty.

Lacy turned to leave. The whole house felt empty. There wasn't a sound except for the running water coming from the bathroom. It suddenly occurred to her that Morgan was the only other person here. She was alone with him.

She gave herself a stern lecture and headed for the kitchen and the promised coffee. So what if they were alone? She'd been at Morgan's place a hundred times and she hadn't thought anything about whether or not they might be alone!

But then again, she'd never been here to refuse a proposal, either.

She'd just poured out two cups and set them on the kitchen table when Morgan appeared in the doorway. He'd removed his shirt and was patting down his bare chest with a towel. "Blasted tractor," he grumbled. "First it broke down. Then when I tried to fix it, it got grease all over me. If I didn't know better, I'd think it had it in for me." He straddled a chair and wiped water from the back of his neck. "So, Lacy, what's on your mind?"

Your chest and your thighs. Lacy struggled for composure. She hadn't expected to be having this conversation with a half-naked man. "I wanted to talk to you about, uh, about what happened yesterday."

"Oh?" Morgan picked up his cup and gave her a look that was so blank she wondered for a minute if he'd forgotten what happened yesterday.

"About what you suggested." His hair was still damp. A few drops of water rolled off it and onto his shoulder, beginning a slow descent through the black pelt on his chest. Lacy dragged her gaze away from them, up to his eyes. "You know. About, uh, the amalgamation of our properties."

"Oh, that." Morgan's expression cleared. "We should discuss that, I suppose." He took a drink of his coffee. "When do you want to do it?"

The trickle of water reached midchest and paused. "Well, I..."

Morgan narrowed his eyes in contemplation. "I was thinking about the later part of August or the early part of September. Somewhere in there."

"August?" The trickle found a path around the black curls and resumed its trip. "That's just over a month away."

"Uh-huh."

"I think it takes longer than that to plan a wedding." She could scoop that drip off him. It would feel cool against her fingertip, but he wouldn't. He'd feel as warm as she was getting. "Janice and Oliver were engaged for a year."

"We can't leave it that long, Lacy."

The drop slid farther down, inching toward his

belt. Lacy watched it, mesmerized, while she struggled to remember the opening line of her prepared speech. "I don't think—"

"We can't." Morgan raised his mug to his lips. "We've got a lot to do...and we want to give your folks plenty of time to get themselves settled before winter hits."

The sparkling droplet of water trickled lower still, trailing across his flat belly. "That's not what—"

"Early September, then?"

"No." The droplet had reached his jeans. He shifted position and it disappeared under his waistband.

"We can't leave it much later than that—although I suppose we could move it up a little, if you're of a mind to do it."

An erotic guess as to the water's final destination flashed through Lacy's brain. She snapped to attention, horrified by her thoughts. What was she thinking about? She wasn't interested in any part of Morgan's anatomy—and she wasn't going to be planning a wedding—ever! *"No!"* she declared again. She raised her head and looked him squarely in the eye. "We're not going to get married, Morgan."

He knitted his brow. "Why not?"

"Because...because it wouldn't be a good idea." She set down her cup. "I mean, I do appreciate your wanting to help us out, but I don't think marriage is the answer."

"I sure as hell can't think of another one." Morgan's features creased with worry. "I really can't, Lacy. I offered Walt a loan, but he wouldn't hear of it."

"Of course he wouldn't. He's too proud for that."

Morgan gestured toward her. "What about you? I could set you up—"

Lacy shook her head. "No. Thank you, but I couldn't do that. I won't go behind Dad's back that way."

Morgan's cup clattered down onto the table. "Well, that's it, then. If you don't marry me, you'll lose the ranch. And you made it real clear the other night that you don't want that to happen."

Lacy recalled the scene in their yard and winced. "I don't. But that doesn't mean you should marry me just so I can keep the ranch. It's kind of you to offer, but it's not necessary."

"It is if you want to keep your ranch."

He had a good point. She didn't have a whole lot of options and she did want to keep her ranch.... "That's not your problem, Morgan. You don't have to sacrifice yourself..." She stopped because he was shaking his head.

"It's not exactly a sacrifice, Lacy. It's about time I was getting married anyway. I'm not getting any younger. And Wade settling down the way he has...well, it does make a man stop and think."

"I guess it would," Lacy agreed, although she didn't see what Wade's trip to the altar had to do with their situation.

Morgan explained it. "The day is going to come when I can't run this place anymore. Who's going to take it over? I don't much care for the idea of some stranger in here."

"I don't like the idea of some stranger at my place, either, but that—"

"Besides, I'm tired of living here by my lonesome. It gets mighty quiet after all the chores are done."

Lacy sat back. Morgan had lived alone here for a number of years. She hadn't thought about how it must be for him. It probably did get lonely. "I can understand your feelings, but that doesn't mean you should marry me."

Morgan drank more coffee. "I might as well. I could use a wife. You need a husband to keep your ranch. It seems to me that this way we can solve both our problems."

It almost made sense—in a weird sort of a way. "That might solve some things but, um, I don't think it's the right solution—for either of us. After all, I'm sure you don't want a marriage of convenience any more than I do."

Morgan blinked. "I don't have a problem with it."

Lacy could have shaken him. "You should, Morgan. I mean, don't you think people should be in love when they get married?"

Morgan shrugged. "I don't see that as necessary. You and I get along tolerably well together. You're smart when it comes to ranching. We both like it. We both know a lot about it. It seems to me that we've got sound, logical reasons for getting married. That's got to be as good as all this romantic nonsense."

He wasn't saying anything that Lacy hadn't thought herself. "Perhaps you do have a point, but—"

"I've got a really good point." Morgan drained his cup, then got to his feet and picked up his shirt. "Look, Lacy, I know I kind of sprung this on you."

He pulled the shirt on over his head. "Maybe you just need a little time to get used to the idea."

Lacy watched as he tugged the shirt down his long torso. "Right," she murmured. "Time. Well, uh…"

"You don't have to make up your mind right now. Why don't you think on it a little? It's not a bad idea. It would help out your folks. You'd be able to keep your ranch. It would solve a lot of problems for both of us."

Lacy tried to come up with a rebuttal, but her brain was preoccupied with the movement of his fingers as he straightened his shirt. "Okay," she heard herself agreeing, "I'll, uh, think about it."

His grin across the table was warm and friendly. "You do that. In the meantime, I've got to get hold of Frank Wilson and see if he can make me up a new hydraulic line for that dadburn tractor of mine."

Lacy wandered out to her truck a few minutes later, feeling as if she'd just been bucked off a horse. What had happened there? Instead of her putting an end to this marriage thing, Morgan almost had her believing it was a good idea!

She drove out of the yard and turned down the gravel road. It wasn't a good idea! Granted, Morgan was a nice enough man, and she was nominally attracted to him, but that didn't mean she should marry him! She didn't want to marry anyone! What she wanted was a big romance with someone exciting—like her ghostly visitor. And she certainly didn't want to get married. She'd end up like Janice, cooking and cleaning, making cookies and wrestling with a sewing machine!

There must be a better way to save her ranch!

EDDIE WAS IN THE BARN, stacking bales of hay, when Morgan ambled in. He straightened and wiped his gloved hands on his jeans. "Was that Lacy's truck I heard pulling out just now?"

Morgan picked up a bale and tossed it onto the stack in the corner. "Yup."

"It's pretty early for stopping in on a neighbor."

"I suppose it is."

Eddie cleared his throat. "There, uh, isn't anything wrong, is there?"

"I wouldn't say that." It had been an odd conversation, though. All that talk about falling in love. He hadn't expected that from levelheaded, sensible Lacy.

Eddie was still watching him. "She didn't catch another sight of that rustler, did she?"

"She didn't mention it."

"How about a ghost?" Eddie chuckled. "Has she seen one again?"

"She didn't mention that, either."

"Oh?" Eddie moved another bale. "She just stopped by for coffee, then?"

"Something like that." Morgan stopped what he was doing to give Eddie the frown he deserved. Eddie was a good hand and his wife made a mean apple pie, but he had a tendency to be nosy that needed to be nipped in the bud. "I gave Frank Wilson a call. He's making up a new hydraulic line for me right now."

Eddie blinked at the sudden change in topic. "That's good."

"How about if you go on in and pick it up?" Morgan suggested. "And while you're at it, you better get another case of oil. I'll finish up here."

"Whatever you say, boss." Eddie tugged a set of keys out of his front pocket and turned to leave.

Morgan watched him go, then returned to his task. He hoped Lacy hadn't seen any more ghosts. Seeing the one had made her act pretty darn peculiar. And that sure had been one peculiar conversation. He'd thought Lacy was too sensible to get all hung up about this falling-in-love business. She'd never shown any indication of wanting to do that before—which was a good thing. Morgan didn't care for the idea of her falling in love with some other guy.

If she was so het up on falling in love, why didn't she fall in love with him? Morgan tossed around a few more hay bales while he considered that idea. It wouldn't bother him if she did that. He recalled the way Wade's wife looked at him—as if he were a steak and she'd been on a chicken diet for a decade. He wouldn't mind if Lacy looked at him that way. He wouldn't mind it at all.

He leaned against the barn door and thought about how she'd looked sitting at his kitchen table, with her brown hair pulled back, her freckled face free of makeup, her lips softly curved in a familiar smile. That was the best thing about Lacy. She was comfortable to be around. She liked talking about the things he liked talking about. She never went off on weird tangents about what they should all wear or what color they should paint the house next. He liked the idea of her being around every day.

And every night. He pictured her in his bed, with her hair spread across his pillow. His body responded to that image. Morgan shook his head at his reaction. He'd been around Lacy for years without taking much notice of her. Now all he had to do was think about her and he got hard. It must be this marriage talk. He was going to have to convince her that they should get married as soon as possible. And if the only way to get her in a church and saying "I do" was to get her to fall in love with him, well, he was going to do it.

It couldn't be that tricky. After all, Wade had managed it. Not that there was anything wrong with Wade, but he'd never been much of a ladies' man. Cassie didn't seem to realize that, though. Hell, she lit up like a candle when he walked into the room. If his brother could get Cassie to fall for him like that, Morgan should be able to get Lacy to do the same thing with him.

He wasn't sure how to do it, though. He'd been with his share of women, mostly from his rodeo days. Those women didn't take a whole lot of romancing. A "Howdy, ma'am" had been sufficient. After that, there hadn't been much talking.

Morgan grinned at the memories, then pushed them out of his mind. He wasn't interested in a quick roll in the hay with Lacy. He thought of her sitting in his kitchen, looking at him with stars in her eyes. That was what he wanted. All he had to do was figure out how to accomplish it.

He sighed deeply and started toward the house. As much as he hated to do it, he was going to have to ask his brother for a little advice.

LACY MIGHT THINK MARRYING Morgan was a dumb
idea, but Janice didn't.

She drove up in her blue-and-silver four by four
that afternoon while Lacy was cleaning out the barn.
Lacy was delighted to see her. After her unsettling
conversation with Morgan, she'd had an equally unsettling one with her parents. She'd tried to explain
that, although she hadn't called off the marriage and
had agreed to think about it, it wasn't exactly a done
deal. They hadn't said much, but the arch looks
they'd given each other, along with their thinly dis-
guised delight, had said it for them. Lacy felt as if
the entire world was lined up against her. She
needed to talk to someone who would understand
how ridiculous this whole thing was.

Janice was definitely not that person. She leaned
her narrow-hipped figure against the barn door,
fluffed out her curly red hair and watched Lacy
shovel a pitchfork full of straw and manure into a
wheelbarrow while she listened to the tale. "You
and Morgan Brillings," she cooed when Lacy finished. "That's so exciting, Lacy! You know, I've always suspected there was something between you
two."

Lacy gave her a disgusted look and stabbed the
pitchfork back into the straw. She should have

known better than to expect Janice to understand how she felt. Janice was married! Married women never understood anything! "There isn't anything between us, Jan. It's one of those marriages of convenience—or in my case, a marriage of *in*convenience!"

"It sounds convenient to me. You'd have your ranch—not to mention Morgan." She pursed her lips. "Are you going to make him wear a tux at the wedding?"

"A tux?" Lacy tried to imagine Morgan in formal attire. "I don't think so."

"Neither do I, although I think he'd look good in one. I insisted Oliver wear one and it was a big mistake. He kept scratching his cummerbund. You can see him do it in all the pictures." Janice tilted her head to one side. "How about you? I think a cream color—in one of those old-fashioned styles with a bustle."

"A bustle!" Lacy shuddered. "I'm not wearing a bustle!"

"Why not? You'd look fabulous. I hope you're going to pick green for your bridesmaids. I look terrific in green." She paused. "I do get to be matron of honor, don't I?"

Lacy rolled her eyes. "If I ever get married, Janice, you can have whatever position you want. But I'm not going to get married."

"But you just said—"

"I said Morgan had suggested it. I didn't say I was going to do it." She set her pitchfork down. "I don't want to get married, thanks. And I'm sure Morgan doesn't want to marry me, either. He just offered to do it to help out our family."

"I don't know about that." Janice nodded thoughtfully. "I think he has a thing for you. I really do."

The idea of Morgan having a "thing" for her made Lacy feel funny. "I don't."

Janice ignored that. "Besides, Morgan should be married. I've always felt a little sorry for him, you know. He's had a pretty lonely life, what with no mother, and Wade for a brother."

Lacy gave her a curious look. "What's wrong with Wade?"

Janice made a face. "Nothing, I suppose—although I've always thought there was something peculiar about him. After all, he did join the navy."

Lacy nodded. Wade's choice of a career had always astonished people. He could have stayed right here and spent his life ranching. Instead, he'd decided to spend it sitting on a boat in the middle of an ocean with nary a cow in sight. There was something odd about that.

"And he's not much of a brother, is he? He's better now that he's gotten married, but before that, he was never around—not even for Christmas." She lowered her voice. "There were times when I don't think Morgan even knew where he was!"

Lacy nodded agreement. Morgan usually spent Christmas with her family—and other holidays, as well. And, on a number of occasions, when someone asked what Wade was up to, Morgan had shrugged and said he hadn't heard from him lately. Come to think of it, Wade *wasn't* much of a brother.

"It would be good for Morgan to have a home and a family of his own," Janice concluded.

Lacy winced as she thought about Morgan's

empty house. "Maybe a family would be good for him, but I'm sure he can find someone else to have it with."

"Why not you? He's a good man. He's got that sexy drawl. Those great thighs. Besides, if you married him, you wouldn't have to work so hard and you'd get to keep your ranch."

"I don't mind the hard work. And there must be a better way of keeping my ranch than getting married!"

Janice opened her hazel eyes in surprise. "What's wrong with getting married?"

"I just don't want to do it. I want to run this ranch myself. I can't do that if I'm married."

"Why not?" Janice wondered. "You do it now."

"I'm not married now. If I get married, I'll have to do all the boring stuff like cooking and cleaning while someone else runs things." She realized that this pretty much described Janice's life. "Not that there's anything wrong with cooking and cleaning but…"

Janice made a face. "I don't blame you. Trust me, cooking and cleaning aren't the high points of my life."

"They aren't?"

"No. But they're all part of making a home with Oliver and that's the high point of my life." She smiled contentedly. "Besides, that's not all I do. I still get to work with the horses when I have time. And Oliver always lets me go on the roundup with them."

Lacy couldn't imagine not going on the roundup. If she got married, she'd have to hope someone would "let" her do it? "Yes, well, that's not what I want."

"It isn't?" Janice looked thoughtful. "I guess I've always known that since you've never made any effort to make it happen." She blinked. "But if that's not what you want, what *do* you want? Aren't you interested in men at all?"

Lacy smiled at the astonished tone in her friend's voice. "Of course I'm interested in men. I just don't want to marry one." Her eyes grew dreamy. "What I'd really like is a torrid romance with a handsome, mysterious stranger."

"A handsome, mysterious stranger, huh?" Janice's eyes glittered with excitement. "You mean someone like Jake Malone."

"Who?"

"Your ghostly gunslinger. Remember?"

"Right." Lacy had almost forgotten about Jake in all the excitement of Morgan's proposal.

"I stopped at the library this morning and found out a lot more about him—and he sounds like just the kind of man you're talking about." She opened her purse and pulled out a couple of sheets of foolscap. "Do you want me to tell you what I learned?"

"I sure do." Lacy set down the pitchfork, pulled off her gloves and rested a shoulder against the stall wall. "Go ahead."

"Okay." Janice quickly scanned her notes. "Jake Malone. Born in Texas sometime in the 1800s. There was no mention of where. He worked all over the Western states as—listen to this—a hired gun."

"A hired gun?" Lacy considered that. There were a lot of negative connotations associated with a hired gun. Then again, in some movies, the hired gun was the good guy. "Is that why he shot that man—because someone paid him to do it?"

"I don't think so. It doesn't sound as if he was that kind of a hired gun. He was more like a—a protector. Ranchers hired him to provide protection from cattle rustlers, fence cutters and land-grabbers."

"Really?" Lacy was more intrigued than ever. "Go on. What was he doing here? What happened to him? What—"

"There isn't much more than that." Janice turned over a page. "According to one book, he showed up in Montana to help a friend defend his silver mine. That was probably somewhere near Carson City." She looked up. "He must have come here after that."

"Why?"

Janice shook her head. "I don't know. Maybe he was just passing through. Then he met Sarah Larkspur."

"He fell for her?" Lacy thought of the strong-looking woman she'd seen in that old photograph yesterday. She didn't look like the type to turn men's heads. As a matter of fact, she looked like the back-to-nature type.

But Janice was shaking her head. "I don't know about that. If he did, nothing came of it. Sarah Larkspur never married."

"Maybe she just had an affair with him." It was so much like her fantasy. A handsome, mysterious stranger shows up out of nowhere, falls for the rancher's daughter. "I don't suppose he was trying to help save her ranch."

"I think he might have been."

Lacy stiffened at that. "What?"

"I'm just guessing." Janice assumed a confidential tone. "I called up Mrs. Kilpatrick to find out what she knew about it. She couldn't tell me much about Jake, but she knew a bit about Sarah. The story is that after Sarah's father passed on, Sarah started having all kinds of problems—hay burned...fences cut...that sort of thing. Then Jake Malone showed up. He and this Karl dude had a gun battle or something and Karl was killed." She folded up the papers. "Sarah didn't have any more problems after that."

"So you think Karl was the one behind all of Sarah's problems?"

"That's what Mrs. Kilpatrick suggested."

"Then Jake came along and shot Karl to help out Sarah." Lacy let her head fall back against the stall and closed her eyes. "He looked like the sort of man who'd do that. I was imagining someone like him right before I saw him."

"Well, you got him."

"Uh-huh." Lacy pictured her good-looking ghost again. "It's too bad he's a ghost. Maybe he could help me out." Not that there was anyone to shoot, but still...

"Ghosts don't show up without a reason, Lacy. Jake Malone was here for a Purpose."

"To haunt me?" Lacy guessed.

"No!" Janice said, looking disgusted. "He'd have to have a better reason than that. He might want you to do something—like avenge his death or find his missing will."

"He died over a hundred years ago, Janice. Isn't that leaving it a little late? Besides, if he wanted me to do something like that, why would he materialize in a pasture? Why wouldn't he show up in a more appropriate place—like a lawyer's office."

Janice's expression grew even more disgusted. "He couldn't do that! Ghosts can only show up in a place they've been to during their lifetime. I'm sure I mentioned that."

"I guess I forgot." Lacy considered that piece of information. "Just a minute. Why would Jake Malone have been on our ranch?"

Janice shrugged. "I don't know. Maybe it used to belong to Sarah Larkspur. You should ask your father about it. He might know something about Jake—or the Larkspurs." She tucked her notes back into her purse. "I don't think the place is as important as the reason he appeared. You know what I think? I think he was trying to tell you something."

"Then why didn't he spit it out instead of disappearing?"

"That's not the way ghosts do things! They don't carry on conversations with people—at least not usually." Janice looked pensive. "Though there was one in Peoria who did spend hours talking to a woman, but he'd been a life insurance salesman. And when someone sees Elvis's ghost, he usually sings a song or two. But that's not their normal behavior."

"I didn't realize ghosts had normal behavior," Lacy muttered. "If they do, my ghost was a normal one because he didn't say a word."

"Most of them don't. Ghosts have a special way of communicating. They use a lot of symbolism. If they're wearing red, it means you're in danger. If they're eating pistachios, it's a sign that you shouldn't go near water. And if they're carrying

money, it means they're trying to tell you about a secret fortune."

"Oh?" A secret fortune sounded good.

Unfortunately, Jake didn't have a cent on him.

IT WAS LATE in the afternoon when Wade returned
Morgan's call.

Morgan was in an owly mood at the time. Eddie
had returned with the part for the tractor but had
forgotten the oil, which meant another trip into
town. Morgan had finished Eddie's chores, then
spent the better part of the day trying to fix the tractor, but with limited success. He was close to finished and thinking fondly of a cold beer when he
heard the phone in the barn ringing. Morgan was
tempted to ignore it—then decided that was a bad
idea. It could be Wade, getting back to him, or it
could be Eddie, calling to find out what he was doing in town this time. Cursing, he dropped his
wrench and caught the phone on the fourth ring.

Fortunately for Eddie, it was Wade. "Brillings
here!" he barked when Morgan picked up the receiver.

Morgan pulled a grease-stained cloth out of his
back pocket and swiped it across his forehead. "Je-
sus, Wade, can't you navy people talk on the phone
the same way normal folks do?"

Wade's chuckle was soft and wry. "Not you, too.
Cassie's always getting after me about that. I've got
no idea what she wants me to say."

"Have you ever considered 'hello'?"

"That just doesn't come natural to me." His voice
sharpened. "What's going on out there?"

"Not a whole lot, but—"

"Must be something. I got a message that you called this morning. I doubt you did that to give me a lecture about my phone manners."

"Not exactly, no." Squatting, Morgan rested his back against the wall. "I wanted to tell you that I'm thinking about getting married."

The brother he'd known for most of his life would have responded with dead silence, along with an unspoken "You called me up just to tell me that?" This brother—the one Wade had turned into after his marriage—was a different man. "Well, don't that beat all!" he exclaimed with clear delight. "That's good news, Morgan. I've got to tell you that I'm glad to hear it. It's about time you settled down. I don't like your being out there on that ranch all by your lonesome. It's been a worry to me."

"It has?"

"Uh-huh. And I know it preys on Cassie's mind, as well. Who is this woman you're thinking of marrying anyway? She's not some floozy, is she?"

"Hell, no. It's Lacy. Lacy Johnson."

"Walt and Rita's daughter? Good choice. She's a fine woman. Can't hold a candle to my Cassie, of course, but I suppose that's a matter of opinion."

His voice held a questionable tone that had Morgan chuckling. Wade figured every man in the galaxy must want to be married to Cassie.

"When are you planning on doing this? It better not be in October. I'm booked up then—although I'll move heaven and earth to be there. I expect you'll want me to stand up for you?"

"As long as you aren't wearing your gun at the time. Folks around here look poorly on that sort of thing. But we haven't set a date. As I said, we're just thinking on it."

"What's there to think about? When a woman you want says she loves you, well, that's the time to get hitched."

Morgan cleared his throat. "That's the problem. Lacy hasn't exactly said that yet."

"What?"

"It's sort of an unusual situation, I suppose." Morgan briefly described his reason for suggesting marriage as well as Lacy's reaction. "She wants to be in love," he concluded.

"That's only to be expected, Morgan." Wade sounded knowledgeable—and a little patronizing. "Women want to be in love before they get married."

Morgan bristled at his tone. Wade liked to think he was an expert on everything. Unfortunately, though, in this case Morgan needed his advice. "Fine," he growled. "You got any idea how I make that happen?"

There was silence, followed by Wade's voice, this time sounding astonishingly close to uncertain. "I don't rightly know. With Cassie, it just sort of...happened. I took her out to dinner, kissed the bejesus out of her—and after that it was pretty close to a done deal."

"Dinner and a kiss, huh?" That sounded good to Morgan—especially the kissing part. "It seems like a good place to start. Anything else?"

"There sure is." The patronizing tone was back in Wade's voice. "I see I better fill you in on a few other things about dealing with women."

WALT WAS SITTING in front of their computer, studying cattle prices, when Lacy approached him about Jake Malone.

"You saw a rustler. I thought we settled that a couple of days ago," he snorted after Lacy told him the whole story.

Lacy didn't feel like arguing with him about it. "Whoever I saw looked exactly like this gunslinger—Jake Malone. Have you ever heard of him?"

"No, I have not."

"What about Sarah Larkspur? Have you heard of her?"

Walt opened his mouth for what Lacy assumed was an automatic no, then hesitated. "Now that you mention it, I suppose I have."

"You have?"

Walt nodded. "I don't know much about her, though. I just recall my dad mentioning the name." He relaxed back into the cushions of the worn black leather chair and rubbed his chin. "I think he said something about his dad getting some of the Larkspur property after the woman who had it passed away."

Lacy felt goose bumps rise on her arms. "Then Janice was right. Sarah's ranch was on our property."

Walt gave her a hard look. "I wouldn't jump to that conclusion. Some of this property has changed hands more than once. I don't rightly know who has that place now. It could be that we're on some of it, and some of it belongs to other folks. Either Morgan or Cal, I expect."

"How about that piece where I saw Jake? Was that—?"

"You didn't see Jake!" His voice rising, Walt straightened in his chair. "You saw a rustler!" He peered at the numbers on his screen. "And I have no idea who owns what now. You'd have to go to the county records office to find that out."

"I just might do that," Lacy muttered. She waited for a moment, but it was clear her father had told her all he was going to tell her. Still, she had found out something. Sarah's land could be on their property—which meant that Jake Malone had once been here, too. She'd sure like to know more about him.

She was just leaving the room when her mother bustled in. "Oh, there you are, Lacy. I've been looking for you."

"You have?"

"Uh-huh." Rita's eyes, so like her own, sparkled with excitement. "Morgan called a little while ago."

Lacy's stomach fluttered. "Oh?"

"Yes. He asked me to tell you that he'll be by to pick you up around six-thirty."

"Pick me up?" Lacy didn't remember arranging to go anywhere with Morgan. It wasn't the right night for the agricultural meeting they both attended. It must be the county rezoning meeting, although she thought that was next month.

"He said he was taking you out to dinner." Rita gave her a curious look. "I didn't realize you two had a date tonight."

"Neither did I." Lacy didn't think Morgan had suggested anything like that this morning. Then again, she'd been so distracted she might not have heard him! "I don't know if I can make it tonight. I have to check on the calves—and there's a broken stall in the barn."

"The world won't end if that isn't fixed tonight," Walt interjected. "And I'm quite capable of taking care of the calves."

"Yes, but, um, I did say I'd help Mom with the pickling."

"I'm not going to make pickles tonight, Lacy. You just go ahead and have a good time. It's been quite a while since you just went out and enjoyed yourself."

Lacy looked from one expectant face to another and gave up. They were right. The work could wait, and it had been a long time since she'd gone out just for fun. The idea was appealing. Besides, it might be a good opportunity to tell Morgan again what a bad idea marriage would be—as long as Morgan kept his shirt on. "Okay, I'll go."

"Good." Rita gave a pointed look at her watch. "Hadn't you better change?"

"Change?"

"Your clothes," Rita prompted. "If Morgan's taking you out to dinner, you shouldn't be dressed like that. And I'm sure you'll want to take a shower."

6

"WHAT TO WEAR, what to wear?" Lacy mused. She stood in front of her closet, her hair wrapped in a towel, and studied her wardrobe. "Will it be jeans and a shirt, jeans and a shirt, or the always lovely jeans and a shirt?"

She shoved around the hangers, but the contents didn't change. There was her going-to-church brown suit, which was too formal, a couple of skirts that hadn't left the closet in months, the peacock blue bridesmaid dress she'd worn for Janice's wedding, and an assortment of jeans, shirts and sweaters.

"It's a good thing I don't have many dates," Lacy muttered. "If I did, I'd have to get a whole new wardrobe."

She pulled out a pair of denims and checked to ensure that the knees were intact. She was not "going out on a date." She was going to grab a bite to eat with Morgan. She'd done that before—just a couple of weeks ago as a matter of fact, when they were on their way home from an auction. This was exactly the same thing. Okay, it didn't feel like the same thing, but it was. They'd probably drive into Silver Spurs and eat at Darlington's restaurant and gas bar. That would be good. People they knew were bound to be there, and they'd end up with a crowd. Right now, a crowd sounded like a good idea.

A crowd wasn't what Morgan had in mind. He was in the living room when she finished dressing, sprawled in a chair while he chatted with her father, looking sexy and unfamiliarly formal in black jeans and a clean white shirt. He'd combed his black hair, his chin showed no five-o'clock shadow, and there was even a faint scent of aftershave clinging to him. He looked as good as he did when he came for Christmas. He rose to his feet when she entered the room and grinned over at her. "Hi, Lacy."

Her pulse picked up speed as she took in his appearance. Now she really wished she owned a more extensive wardrobe—or had made more of an effort to dress up. "Hi, Morgan," she said, feeling unusually shy. "Don't let me interrupt your conversation. We don't have to leave right now."

"Might as well." Morgan picked up his hat. "It's a bit of a drive to Cattle Creek."

"Cattle Creek? But that's thirty miles away."

"That's not a problem, is it?"

Lacy gave her parents a weak smile and headed out the door. One evening, that's all. She'd spend one evening with him. Maybe that would satisfy her parents.

Morgan opened the door of his truck for her and Lacy self-consciously climbed in. She couldn't recall the last time anyone had opened a door for her—or closed it for her, either. She rather liked it, although it did emphasize the change in their relationship. Before all this marriage talk, Morgan had never done anything like that.

She leaned against the door and watched as he

wheeled the truck onto the highway. There were a lot of things about him she hadn't noticed before. The stretch of his jeans as he pressed on the gas. The curl of his fingers around the gearshift. The strong column of his throat. The black-and-brown mixture of chest hair peeking out from the top of his shirt. The scents of aftershave, soap and male wafting through the cab. They all mingled together in her brain, causing her body to fill with a now familiar, and extremely unwelcome, ache.

The miles rolled by. Morgan made a couple of comments about the weather, then fell silent, apparently content to drive along without saying anything. Lacy's fascination with his body parts and muscle groups continued to grow. Say something, she ordered herself. Pick a topic of conversation. Cattle. Grazing methods. Anything to get your mind off his body.

She searched her brain for a subject, but it wasn't functioning properly. She couldn't even remember how she usually started a conversation with Morgan. "Did you get your tractor fixed?" she finally said.

"Uh-huh." He made a face. "It took the better part of the day to do it, though. I've got to tell you, Lacy, I'd much rather work with cattle than fix machines. At least with a cow you don't have to spend hours stretched out over an engine."

"It took all day?" An image of how he'd look splayed across the tractor sprang into Lacy's mind. If she'd known he was going to spend a whole day like that, she might have hung around.

"Uh huh." He slanted her a sideways look. "How about yourself? What have you been up to?"

"Not much." Lacy tried to banish the image from her mind. "Janice Delany stopped by." The reason for Janice's visit came back to her. Lacy latched on to it. She didn't expect Morgan to believe her, but at least it would give her something else to think about. "You remember that ghost I saw?"

Morgan half smiled. "I sure do, honey. Not something I'm likely to forget."

Lacy chose to ignore that. "Well, I know whose ghost it was."

"How's that?"

"He was a gunslinger named Jake Malone."

YOU'VE BEEN OUT *in the sun too long.*

That was the first thing that came into Morgan's mind when Lacy started telling him about this Jake Malone. Either that or she was suffering from a severe case of women's hormones and she'd lost her common sense.

She was still going on about it when they reached the restaurant. "...then Janice brought out Mrs. Kilpatrick's book on the history of the area," she enthused. "And there he was."

Morgan took a quick look at her as he pulled into a parking space, wondering if maybe she was putting him on. She wasn't. Her expression was perfectly serious. She really believed this nonsense.

He opened his mouth to ask her why in hell she was acting this way, then closed it again as he remembered his brother's advice. "When a woman tells you something that sounds peculiar, you're best off believing them. They get mighty testy when you tell them they're acting irrationally...and sometimes it turns out that they're right."

Morgan knew for a fact that Lacy was dead wrong about this. For one thing, he found the existence of ghosts mighty difficult to swallow. For another, if they did exist, well, surely they had better things to do than lurk around a fairly deserted stretch of grazing land, with nothing to haunt other than a few cows. However, there was something about the set of Lacy's jaw that suggested if he did tell her she was losing it, she would get testy. He didn't want to start an argument with her about it—not tonight at any rate. After they were married, well, then he would do something about it. Right now, it didn't seem as important as sharing a meal and some quiet conversation with her and coaxing her along the road to falling in love with him.

"Jake Malone," he said. "I don't recall hearing that name before."

"I hadn't heard about him, either, until I saw his picture in that book. He's a really interesting character, Morgan." She went on eagerly to explain about Jake. Morgan stretched back and let her talk. It was all nonsense of course, but as he took in her freckled face, her pink lips, the smooth, tanned column of her throat, he decided he didn't much care. Lacy was looking good tonight. She usually had her hair tied back, but tonight it floated around her shoulders in golden brown waves, curling where it touched her cheek. Her green eyes sparkled as she talked. She wasn't movie-star beautiful, but she was a fine looking woman, and he was enjoying being out with her. That was all that mattered.

He realized Lacy had stopped talking and made an effort to keep up his end of the conversation. "So this Malone character came to town, shot some guy and rode out again?"

"Not exactly. I don't really know for certain what he was doing here or why he shot that guy—Karl…Robinson, I think. But he could have done it to help out Sarah."

"Sarah?"

"Sarah Larkspur. Janice couldn't find out a lot, but what she did learn suggests that Jake had to shoot that guy—to save Sarah's ranch for her."

"Who was this guy?"

"I don't know anything much about him. All Janice could discover was that his name was Karl Robinson and he ranched up here. Have you ever heard of him?"

Morgan shook his head. "I can't say that I have, no. Unless he's related to Cal Robinson."

"Cal?"

"Yeah. It seems to me that Cal mentioned he had some long-gone relation who was killed in a gun battle back in the old days. Maybe it was this Karl character."

Lacy's eyes lit up. "Maybe it was. Maybe Cal knows something about it."

"Could be." Morgan's faint interest in Lacy's gunslinger faded. "Listen, Lacy, I think we need to talk a little more about this marriage business."

"Marriage?" Lacy blinked rapidly as if to bring herself back to the present. "Oh, yes, that. I wanted to talk to you about that, too." She glanced around and lowered her voice. "You haven't, uh, mentioned it to anyone, have you?"

"Just Wade. I told him I'd suggested it and that you were thinking on it."

"What did he say?"

"He was all for it." Morgan chuckled. "So was his wife. Cassie called me up as soon as Wade filled her in. She said she wasn't one bit surprised. She figured there was something between us the minute she met you."

"She did?"

"Uh-huh." Morgan thought of the incomprehensible conversation he'd had with his sister-in-law. "You're going to have to watch out for her. She's already designing a wedding dress. Kept asking me questions about it. I finally told her to talk to you."

"Did you?" Lacy cleared her throat. "You know, Morgan, I'm not like Cassie. For one thing, I don't know how to sew."

"Thank God for that," Morgan mumbled.

"What?"

"That woman drives me half-crazy." He raised a hand. "Don't get me wrong now. I like Cassie well enough. She's a decent person and she's been good for Wade. But she's got some mighty peculiar notions. She's always telling Wade what to wear—and last time she was out she started in on me."

Lacy's shoulders shook. "She did?"

"Darn right she did. And look at the way she tore into my place. Now, I'm not saying it didn't need a little work, but every time she visits, she wants to redecorate!" He frowned. "You're not going to start wanting to do that when you move in, are you?"

Lacy looked surprised. "Good heavens, no!" She paused. "What do you mean, when I move in?"

"After we're married, you'd move into my place."

"I haven't decided if we're going to get married." Lacy stabbed her fork into a piece of meat. "But if we did, why would we move into your place? Why wouldn't we move into mine?"

Morgan had assumed she understood the future living arrangements. "Of course we'll live at my place. When a woman marries a man, she always moves into his place. That's the way things are done."

Lacy set down her water glass. "There's no rule that says it has to be done that way."

"I suppose there isn't." Morgan stretched back and gave the matter some thought. They didn't have to live on his ranch, he conceded, although it was what he wanted—her there, with a few kids to fill up the empty rooms. "But my house is a lot bigger than your folks' place. It only makes sense for us to live there."

"I guess it does, but...but what about my place? What would we do with it if we didn't live there? My parents want to move into town."

"How about if Eddie moves in there? I'm sure he and Susan would like it better than that trailer they're in now."

Lacy scowled. "I don't know if I like the idea of other people living there."

"Then we'll leave it empty!"

"I don't like that idea, either. Besides, what about all our cattle? Who's going to take care of them?"

"We are," Morgan said, puzzled by the question. "We could put together a mighty fine herd if we combined our livestock."

Lacy's eyes flickered with interest. "I suppose we could."

"If we handled the land properly, we could raise a lot more cattle. Or we could just keep things the way they are and look into getting some of those exotic breeds. I've always had a notion to do something like that."

"So have I." He definitely had her attention now. "I wouldn't mind raising some rodeo stock—and maybe bringing in some of those Japanese cattle I've been reading about. Of course, Dad would never hear of it, but—"

"I'm all for it," Morgan said immediately. He'd never considered Japanese stock, but if that's what she wanted, he sure was all for it.

She beamed at him. "Really?"

"Uh-huh. Now I've been thinking..."

He went on to discuss his plans. Lacy joined right in, arguing with him, sometimes agreeing, sometimes coming up with ideas of her own. Morgan gave himself a mental pat on the back. This was going just fine. Lacy had started out a little testy and that ghost business had been a surprise, but at least she was talking about this marriage as if it had some chance of happening. He had to give it to his brother. Wade knew a lot more about women than Morgan had given him credit for.

IT WAS PAST MIDNIGHT when Morgan stopped his truck in front of Lacy's house. "Here we are," he said as he switched off the engine.

Lacy looked around, surprised. It was a thirty-minute drive back from the city. She'd been so caught up in the discussion that she hadn't noticed. Morgan climbed out. Lacy picked up her purse and started to open her own door, but Morgan was already there, opening it for her and helping her out.

She smiled up at him as they walked toward the

house together. "This has been great. I don't know when I've had such a good time."

Morgan stopped at the door and grinned down at her. "I enjoyed it myself."

Lacy suddenly felt awkward. She put her hand on the door handle. "Would you like to come in for coffee, or…?"

"Nope. It's a little late. I like to get some shut-eye before the critters realize it's morning."

"Oh." He was still standing there, his eyes gleaming at her. Lacy's pulse gave a nervous flutter. "Well, uh, good night, then."

Morgan's lips curled into a slow smile. "I don't think that's how two people contemplating marriage should say good-night."

Lacy swallowed. "You don't?"

"Nope. I think it's more like this." He clamped an arm around her waist and swooped her up against the solid wall of his body. Then he lowered his head and planted his mouth squarely over hers.

It wasn't a subtle kiss by any means. Even with her limited experience in romance, Lacy knew that. There was little finesse in it. Morgan kissed the way he did everything else—in a straight, no-nonsense manner that hit Lacy with the force of a two-ton bull. The second their lips met, a current of pure electricity jolted through her, shocking her so much that for an instant she did nothing but stand there.

Morgan's hand moved into her hair, holding her head where he wanted it, while the other kept her firmly against him. His lips moved over hers, the pressure of them as compelling as the feel of his body. Without a thought, without making any conscious decision to do so, Lacy's arms moved to circle his neck, and she was kissing him back. He tasted like coffee and apple pie, and he felt even better.

Lacy sagged against him, opening her mouth under his. It had been some time since she'd kissed a man. She'd almost forgotten what it felt like to be pressed against a hard, masculine body, to have a man's lips travel over hers. She hadn't thought about it in a long time, but it was all coming back to her. And while she was feeling all those things, she was aware of other parts of him—distinctly masculine parts that pushed against her aching, feminine ones. More, she thought vaguely. She wanted more. She thrust her hips forward. His thigh moved, inserting itself between her legs as if it had every right to be there. She gasped her pleasure into his mouth and clutched him more tightly, using her tongue to get a better taste of him, rubbing herself against him.

Morgan released her. "We'd better stop that, honey, or Walt will be out here with a shotgun."

Lacy staggered backward and stared up at him in wide-eyed astonishment. She never would have guessed that kissing Morgan could feel so good.

Morgan chuckled and gave her cheek a proprietary pat. "Good night, Lacy." He grinned a smart, pleased-with-himself grin, nodded his head and headed toward his truck. Lacy stood there, staring after him. She'd just given her fuzzy head a shake and was starting to open the door when he called after her. "Lacy?"

She turned. "Hmmm?"

"How about if you drop by my place tomorrow? You can take a look around and we can finish discussing how we're going to manage two herds of cattle."

Lacy was too stunned to think. "Okay."

"About four?"

"All right."

"I'll see you then." He climbed into his truck and drove off. Lacy watched him leave while her body temperature gradually lowered to somewhere close to normal. It wasn't Walt's shotgun he had to worry about. If he kissed her like that again, she might go after him with one herself—only it wouldn't be marriage she had in mind.

MORGAN HUMMED ALONG with the radio as he drove home. This thing with Lacy was progressing nicely—except for the ghost nonsense, that is.

He slowed to take the turn toward his ranch, a small frown sliding across his brow as he thought about that. First there was a ghost and then she'd found a name for him. Who would have thought Lacy would dream up something like that? Granted, this Jake Malone sounded like a pretty intriguing character, but he didn't understand Lacy's fascination with him. He'd shot a man, for chrissake. That wasn't an admirable character trait. On the other hand, Lacy made it sound as if he'd done it to help out that Larkspur woman—the one who'd been having all those problems. Fences cut. Cattle being poisoned.

Sort of like the things that had been happening to the Johnsons.

Morgan opened his window to let in some cool night air and hopefully a little common sense. What was he thinking? Granted, the Johnsons had experienced a lot of bad luck, but that was nothing like what had happened to the Larkspurs. That Karl character had been trying to force them off their land. No one was trying to force the Johnsons off theirs! He was just getting too caught up in Lacy's tale. After they were married, he'd put an end to this foolishness.

He felt his lips move into a slow smile at the thought of marrying her. After that kiss, he was more anxious than ever to get it settled. It shouldn't take too long. By the end of the week, they'd be engaged and could have the wedding next month. Then they could start working on amalgamating their properties.

But it wasn't their livestock that occupied his thoughts as he guided his truck through the darkness and it wasn't Lacy's gunslinger, either. It was the way she'd looked sitting across from him, the sensation of her soft lips opening under his and the inviting warmth of her body.

7

"I DON'T KNOW WHY we called this meal breakfast," Lacy grumbled the next morning. She scraped the remnants of pancakes and sausages into the garbage and carried her plate over to the sink. "We should just refer to it as an interrogation session during which food is served."

Her mother just laughed. She was looking much better than she had yesterday morning, Lacy noted. The good humor was back in her face and the curve of her lips hinted at a teasing smile. "We're not interrogating you. We just asked a couple of questions about your evening."

"A couple of questions?" Lacy snorted. "You've asked more than a couple of questions! So far you've wanted to know where we went, what time we got there, if we saw anybody we knew, what I ate, what Morgan ate, what we talked about and how late I got home!"

Her father rocked back in his chair. "You don't often have dates, Lacy. We weren't real sure you remembered how to do it." He chuckled and winked at his wife.

Disgusted with both of them, Lacy shook her head. "It wasn't exactly a date. It was more like a...a meeting." A meeting that had ended with one whopper of a kiss. She hadn't thought Morgan would be such a good kisser. Then again, until recently she hadn't thought about kissing him at all.

"Of course," Rita said. "A meeting." Her tone led Lacy to give her a quick, over-the-shoulder glance. There was a small, knowing smile on Rita's face as she gathered up the dishes. Lacy flushed. Her parents had been in bed when she'd come in last night, but judging from their behavior she had a strong suspicion they knew all about that kiss. Resisting the urge to do something childish like stomping her foot, she turned back to the sink. At least her mother was trying to be tactful.

Her father wasn't. "A meeting?" he snorted as he got to his feet. "I don't recall Morgan kissing anyone like that when we were at the Cattlemen's Association meeting last month. If he's going to start kissing folks like that after a meeting, maybe I should start packing my shotgun."

"Dad!"

"Just want to protect myself, Lacy." He grinned, then sauntered out of the room.

Lacy scowled at his back, then faced her mother. "You two weren't spying on me, were you?"

"No," Rita said. "At least, I wasn't. Your father did take a look out the window when you drove up. I stayed in bed and told him not to do it." She smiled, her eyes twinkling. "Of course, I made him tell me every single detail."

"Mother!"

"It's part of a parent's duty, Lacy."

Smiling, Lacy shook her head. It was impossible to stay mad at her mother for long. Besides, she couldn't really blame her parents. If she was in their shoes, she probably would have done the same thing. "Just don't read too much into it," she warned as she began setting plates in the dishwasher. "It didn't mean anything. It was more like an...an experiment."

"Of course, dear." Rita picked up a cloth and began wiping the table. "Are you, um, going to be seeing Morgan again?"

"I imagine so." Lacy turned back to the sink to collect more plates. "We're always stumbling across Morgan one way or another."

"That's true, I guess." Rita sounded amused. "I was just asking because Heather Norfolk called last night to invite us over for dinner and cards this evening. I told her I wasn't sure if you'd be able to join us."

Lacy made a face. She didn't mind the Norfolks, but Heather did have a tendency to go on and on about how Lacy should get married and raise a few dozen children. "I don't think I can, thanks. I've got a lot of things to do around here. And I want to stop by Cal's place to see if he knows anything about Jake Malone. Morgan suggested it might have been one of his ancestors that Jake shot."

"You told Morgan about that?"

"Uh-huh." Lacy didn't think Morgan had believed much of her ghost story, but he hadn't dismissed it, either. He'd just sat there, listening to her, sometimes smiling, sometimes frowning, looking as delicious as the steak she'd been eating. She had a sudden recollection of their last conversation. "Oh, I almost forgot. I told Morgan I'd stop by later."

Rita gave her an arch look. "You're going to Morgan's place, are you?"

"Yes." To her horror, Lacy felt herself blush. "It's

not a date or anything. I just said I'd go over there to, uh, take a look around."

"Ah," Rita said, looking wise. "Well, be sure to check out his fridge."

"His *fridge*?" Lacy blinked. "That's a new word for it."

Rita giggled. "I meant his refrigerator, Lacy." She wrinkled her nose. "It's so old it's practically an antique. And there isn't room for anything in it. I certainly couldn't cope with it."

The warmth in Lacy's cheeks spread to the tips of her ears. "I'm not planning on coping with Morgan's fridge—or anything else."

"Uh-huh."

"I'm not. This doesn't *mean* anything! We just starting talking about things last night. You know. In general."

"Uh-huh."

"And Morgan's got the idea that if we were married, we'd live in his house! He even suggested that Eddie and Susan move in here."

Rita wiped table crumbs into her hand. "That sounds like a practical idea."

Lacy stared at her. She'd expected her mother to be horrified by the idea. She'd even thought that perhaps if her parents knew about Morgan's plans, they'd be less inclined to support their marriage. Perhaps her mother just didn't get it. "Doesn't the idea of strangers living in your house bother you?"

"Eddie and Susan aren't strangers." Rita dumped the crumbs into the garbage and dusted her hands. "I practically grew up with Susan's mother. As for Eddie—well, he used to be something of a hellraiser, but he seems to have his life straightened around now. I think they'd be very happy here."

"I think I'd be very happy here," Lacy muttered under her breath. "Don't get your heart set on Eddie and Susan moving in. It was just talk, that's all."

"That's what you and Morgan were doing out there last night? Talking?"

Lacy rolled her eyes. Her parents were acting as if things were all settled just because she'd shared a meal with Morgan! If they acted this way after one date, what would they do if she spent the night with him? Visions of a shotgun wedding, with the gun pointed at the bride, flashed through her head. Then she remembered that hot kiss. Maybe that gun wouldn't be necessary after all.

Of course it would! Just because she liked kissing him didn't mean she wanted to spend the rest of her life with him. Her reaction to that kiss was only natural. It had been a long time since she kissed anyone besides her parents and her horse.

She replayed that kiss one more time, then ordered it out of her mind. It had been an experiment, that's all, and one that wasn't going to be repeated. Still, as she grabbed her hat and headed out to start on the chores, she had to admit that if having a torrid affair with Morgan Brillings would solve her problems, she might be more agreeable.

CAL ROBINSON DIDN'T believe in ghosts, either—but at least he was nice about it.

He sat on the flowered couch in his living room, a large distinguished-looking, blunt-faced man in his early fifties, with graying hair and soft brown eyes.

"Jake Malone, huh? That's the name of that ghost you think you saw?"

"That's right." Lacy had anticipated his reaction and refused to let it bother her. She even found herself smiling back at him. She'd always found it difficult to resist Cal's good humor. "I saw his picture in the area history book and I recognized him right away."

"Well, don't that beat all. Does Walt know about this?"

"Uh-huh. So does Morgan. He's the one who told me that Karl Robinson might be related to you. He's the man Jake shot, I believe."

"Karl Robinson?" Cal frowned and looked doubtful. "I don't know about that. My mother did say that some great-uncle of hers was killed in a gun battle, but I never gave much credence to it. I always thought that was just a story my mother liked to tell. One of those women things."

"Women things?" What was it with the men around here? Did they all think every woman went around imagining gunslingers and shoot-outs?

"I couldn't say if it was true or not," Cal concluded.

His expression indicated he wasn't particularly interested in it, either. Lacy decided to abandon Jake and try for Sarah. "What about the Larkspurs?"

"Hmm." Cal scratched the back of his head. "Name doesn't ring a bell."

"They were supposed to have ranched around here a long time ago. Dad thought their place might be on our property now."

Cal still looked blank. "I wouldn't know about that."

"Oh." Clearly, Cal wasn't going to be any more help than her father. Lacy started to rise. "It doesn't really matter. I can always check at the county office. They should have some records."

"There's no need for that." Cal got to his feet. "I've got an old map of the area. Why don't we take a look at it?" He want down the hall and came back a few minutes later with a rolled-up map clutched in his hand. He sat down beside her, spread it out on the coffee table and stared down at it. "What was that name again?"

"Larkspur." Lacy leaned forward, trying to read the small printing.

"Ah, yes, Larkspur. Here it is." Cal put a meaty finger on the map. "'Larkspur.' It looks like it's mostly on my land now."

"Oh." He was right. The boundaries of his property did include the former Larkspur ranch. Lacy studied it, disappointed. "Are you sure this map is accurate?"

"It sure is, Lacy. I got a copy of it from the county office a couple of years back." He rolled the map back up. "Was there anything else you wanted to know?"

"No." Lacy rose to her feet. If the Larkspur ranch was on Cal's property, what was Jake doing on her land? It didn't make sense.

"I'm sorry I wasn't more help," Cal said as they left the room.

"It's not really important, I suppose. And I appreciate your taking the time to discuss it with me."

"No problem at all. It's always a pleasure seeing you." He opened the front door, then paused. "How's your father feeling these days?"

"He's fine. Oh, he tires a lot more easily than he used to, but don't tell him I said so. Apart from that, he's doing okay."

"That's good to hear. Then there's no truth to the rumor that he's thinking of selling out?"

"Absolutely not," Lacy lied. "Oh, he and Mom will probably move into town one of these days, but when that happens, I'll take over."

"You?" Cal chuckled. "You can't be planning on taking over that place all by yourself."

"I certainly am!"

Cal still looked amused. "You can't do that, Lacy."

"Of course I can! Why shouldn't I? I've been pretty much running the place for the past few years. I'm quite capable of managing it by myself."

"I'm sure you are but…well, you're a woman. I'm sure you'll be taking off one of these days to get married."

Not him, too! It seemed as if half the county—the male half—was trying to marry her off and take her ranch away from her. Lacy stuck out her chin. "I am not taking off anywhere!" She yanked open the door of her truck. "And I have no intention of getting married."

IT WAS TWENTY MINUTES after four when Lacy's old red truck pulled up in front of Morgan's house.

Morgan was relieved to see it. He'd been loitering around the barn for a good hour, checking his watch every so often and wondering if she'd changed her mind about coming. He knew it was ridiculous. After all, when people said they'd be there around four, that could mean any time between two and eight. Still, he felt as if a weight had been lifted off his shoulders when she appeared.

She wheeled the truck to a teeth-rattling stop in front of his house. Morgan winced at the squeal of brakes. He was going to have to give her a quick course on how to treat a vehicle before the wedding. He didn't want her handling his truck the way she did hers.

She wrenched open the door, and Morgan winced again. It might be best if he just made sure she always had her own vehicle to drive. "Hi, Lacy. How you doing?"

"Just fine." She jumped to the ground, then gave the door a slam that had him grimacing.

Taking in her flushed face and flashing eyes, he realized something was amiss. "Is anything wrong?"

"It's just Cal, that's all. Sometimes he can really get on my nerves."

"You saw Cal today?" Morgan guessed.

"Uh-huh. I stopped by his place to ask him about Jake."

She was wearing a pale pink shirt, tucked into a pair of faded jeans, her hair was tied back from her freckled face, and her green eyes gleamed with annoyance. Morgan lost his place in the conversation. "Jake?"

"Jake Malone. That ghost I saw."

"Oh, yeah." Morgan had almost forgotten about him. "You, uh, told Cal about that?"

Lacy nodded. "You suggested Karl Robinson might be related to him. You know—the guy Jake shot. I went to Cal's place to see if he knew anything about it."

Morgan had a vague recollection of saying something like that, but he hadn't expected Lacy to use that as a reason to go tearing around the county, asking questions about her mythical ghost. He was pretty sure he could guess Cal's reaction—which gave him a sudden insight into Lacy's mood. "What did Cal have to say about it?"

"Not much." Lacy looked disgusted. "I don't understand it. If my great-great-uncle had been shot by a gunslinger, I'd know a lot more about it than he does. Not only doesn't he know anything about it, he doesn't seem to care if he knows anything about it."

"He probably doesn't think it's of much importance," Morgan grumbled back. He didn't feel like talking about Lacy's gunslinger today, either. He wanted to talk about her moving into his house.

And into his bedroom.

He took a breath. "Where do you want to start? Do you want to have a look out here first before we go inside?"

"Whatever you like." She didn't sound as interested as she had last night, Morgan realized. He took her arm, inhaled her distinctly Lacy scent and devoted himself to rekindling that interest.

Half an hour later, he was sure he'd done it. He'd given her the deluxe tour, showing her all the outbuildings, including the grain storage sheds, the shop where they did the mechanical work, all the equipment, and he'd even led her through the barn. "There's lots of room for those Japanese cattle you were talking about," he explained as they stood beside one of the corrals.

"There is, isn't there?" Her eyes grew dreamy. "I

can just imagine how they'd look—a bunch of little cows grazing alongside the others."

Morgan took in the expression on her face and clenched his teeth. Wade's wife got that look whenever Wade's name was mentioned. However, it seemed Lacy only looked like that when she was talking about cattle…or ghosts.

Lacy stopped beside her truck and started to open the door. "I'd better get back."

"Not just yet." He gestured toward the house. "Don't you want to have a look inside, too?"

"That's not necessary. I've seen your house." She paused. "Although Mom did mention something about your fridge. I suppose I'd better check it out."

"The fridge?"

Lacy shrugged. "I don't understand it, either. I think it's some sort of mother thing."

Morgan didn't care what kind of thing it was as long as she hung around. He took her back to the house and put on a pot of coffee while Lacy examined his fridge.

"I don't know what Mom was talking about. It seems fine to me." She opened the door and peered inside. "It is a little on the small side, though. And it does look like it's a million years old. How long have you had it?"

"I'm not real sure. Could be my great-great-grandfather brought it here right after the end of the Civil War."

She laughed. "You might just be right about that." She pursed her lips while considering the rest of the kitchen. "The stove looks a lot newer."

"It is. I bought it a couple of years ago."

"What about the dishwasher?" She looked

around. "Come to think of it, where is the dish-washer?"

"I don't have one."

Lacy's eyes widened. "You don't have a *dish-washer?*"

Morgan felt a tad embarrassed at his lack of appliances. "No, I don't."

"Haven't you *ever* had one?"

"No!" Now he felt defensive. "You should know that. You've been here plenty of times before."

"Yes, but I wasn't looking for a dishwasher then!" She put her hands on her hips. "How can anyone survive in this day and age without a dishwasher?"

Morgan didn't consider a dishwasher a necessity. "I guess I'm just the hardy type. But if you want one, we can always get one."

"We'll have to, Morgan! I'm not going to wash dishes by hand, thanks!" Her eyebrows lowered as she studied the situation. "We could build it in here, beside the sink—though we'd lose a lot of cupboard space. But we could compensate for that if we put in an island."

Morgan had no idea what she was talking about, but he didn't care. He was enjoying her use of the word "we." He settled back and let her ramble on about building in more cupboards—maybe even re-modeling the whole room. Just having her sitting in his house brightened up the place.

If she looked this good in a kitchen, think what she'd do for a bedroom. Morgan got to his feet, unable to resist the lure of that tantalizing image. "I suppose you'll want to go on upstairs, as well?"

Lacy hesitated. "I don't really have to...."

"You came to check the place out, Lacy. You should see everything."

He took her arm, propelled her down the hall and up the stairs, admiring the sway of her denim-encased hips. The woman could sure fill out a pair of jeans. How come he'd never noticed that before?

The second floor consisted of a long hallway, with four bedrooms and a bathroom opening off either side of it. "This one here is the spare room," he said, gesturing to the one on the right. "Wade and Cassie use it when they come to visit. And there are a couple more rooms down the hall. They haven't been used for years. I figure they'd be good rooms for the kids." He stopped at the doorway to one of them—the one he'd used when he was young—and pictured the room with his child in it.

He was so caught up in his thoughts that he almost jumped when Lacy spoke. "There's no way we're putting any kids in here unless we do something with it."

Morgan straightened and glanced around with mild surprise. The room seemed much the same as it had when he'd occupied it—a plain single bed, an old wooden dresser that had been in the house as long as he could remember, and not much else. "What's wrong with it?"

"It's too...drab."

"Drab?"

"And dark. And those curtains..." She shook her head. "I don't mean to be rude, but those curtains have got to go."

Morgan eyed the curtains. They'd always been in this room as far as he knew. He wasn't that fond of them, but... "What's wrong with them?"

"They're falling apart—plus they're the ugliest color I've ever seen." She crossed the room to finger them, her nose wrinkling in disgust. "I don't know even know what you'd call the color. It's either cow-pie brown or muddy yellow." She glanced at the bed and made another face. "And they don't go with that old green bedspread."

"They don't?" Morgan said, not getting it.

"No. Besides, no one around here uses bed-spreads anymore. Everyone has quilts."

"Quilts?" Morgan furrowed his brow. "I don't see what difference it makes what the bedspread looks like. It's not as if the whole county traipses through my bedrooms."

"That's a good thing," Lacy grumbled. "I'll have to get my mother over here. She made lovely cur-tains for my room last year. And I've got some quilts my grandmother made me that would be perfect in here."

Morgan couldn't believe his ears. Was he really having this conversation with Lacy? It was more the sort of conversation he'd expect to have with Wade's wife. He shuddered. Were paint samples re-ally looming in his future?

"I'd better see the other rooms," Lacy announced. She squeezed past him and marched down the hall.

Morgan rolled his eyes and followed. Wade was right. It wasn't just Cassie. It was women. They were all like that.

Lacy was just as disapproving of the other unused bedroom. "You should have done something about these a long time ago," she scolded. "Both rooms need a lot of work." She stopped at the door to the room Morgan occupied now. "This one is much better."

Morgan glanced around, unacceptably pleased by her praise. He'd moved in here years ago, long after his father passed away. It was a wide square room, painted in beige, with dark blue curtains Lacy's mother had made for him. A blue-and-gold blanket covered the bed, an ancient chest stood at the end of it, and apart from a plain wooden dresser, there wasn't much else. "This will be our bedroom," he advised.

Lacy turned around. "What?"

"This will be our room." He opened the closet to show her the expanse of empty space. "There's plenty of room here for your things."

"Oh." Lacy glanced up at him. A few strands of hair had come loose from their fastenings and curled around the edge of her flushed face. Her lips were softly curved, her eyes wide and luminous as they met his. "Of course. Our bedroom."

She looked at the bed and then at him. Damn, but he couldn't help picturing her stretched out on it, her golden brown hair spreading lustrously across the whiteness of the pillow. Morgan recalled the firm feel of her small breasts against his chest, the softness of her lips parting eagerly under his, the sensation of her thighs pressing on his own. As surely as if she'd spoken the words, he knew she was thinking the same thing.

Lacy turned to the window. "These curtains aren't too bad," she said.

Morgan put a hand on her shoulder and pulled her gently to face him. "Forget the curtains, Lacy."

She stared up at him with round, glowing eyes.

Then she was plastered against him, her hands coming up to circle his neck, pulling his head down as hers came up. His lips fastened over hers. She moaned into his mouth, the small sound echoing through his brain so that all he could think about was her...the feel of her, the scent of her, the taste of her. She arched back, her breasts straining against his chest. The sensation of her nipples hardening in desire was unbelievably erotic. He raised his head for a breath, then kissed her again while his hand stroked up her torso, closing around a small, round breast.

Lacy shuddered.

That was all the encouragement Morgan needed. He kissed the corner of her mouth, then traced his lips across her jawline and on into the curve of her throat. She panted into his ear, heavy, lustful gasps that matched his own harsh breathing. Her head dropped to one side, allowing him access to her soft neck. His fingers left her breast, seeking and finally finding the buttons of her shirt. He worked them open with clumsy haste, pressing his lips against her skin while he pushed away the material and groped inside, eager to feel her. He touched the edge of her bra, then eased it down. Her breast tumbled free into his palm. He studied the creamy flesh, fascinated by the contrast against his dark tan. His thumb moved along the gentle curve, then touched the tight, pink nipple.

Lacy sucked in her breath and raised her eyelids slowly, languorously, as if they were almost too heavy to move. Her eyes, when he could see them, were wide and dazed. For a second, they just stared at one another. Then she gasped and jerked away.

The motion was so sudden and so unexpected that it took Morgan a good ten seconds to realize what had happened. He gave his head a shake to clear it, struggled with the impatient demands of his own body, then focused on Lacy.

She was standing out of arm's reach, fumbling with her clothing. Morgan almost groaned out loud as he saw the creamy skin of her breast disappear into her shirt. He took a step toward her. "Lacy...?"

"I, uh, I really should be going," Lacy stammered. She whirled past him and was out the bedroom door before Morgan knew what she was doing.

Morgan swore under his breath, rearranged his jeans over his aching member and followed her down the stairs. Lacy was in the front hall tugging on her boots when he caught up with her. Her face was hidden behind a curtain of brown hair. Morgan watched her for a moment, then cleared his throat, searching for something to say. "There's no need to run off, Lacy."

"I'm not running off." She flicked back her hair and gave him a totally false smile, her eyes not quite meeting his. "I have to get home, that's all. There're chores to do...and Mom gets worried if I'm away too long and...and...uh..." She fished her keys out of her jeans pocket. "And I'd better just go."

She flew out the door. Morgan watched the screen slam behind her and shook his head. It had to be those goddamn hormones again. Hadn't they invented something to control those yet?

8

LACY HAD ANTICIPATED another interrogation session over breakfast the next day, but a series of small emergencies—one of the calves took sick, the pump got stopped up, and Intrigue jumped the fence—kept everyone busy. So it was almost lunchtime when her father told her that the danger from rustlers was pretty much in the past.

Walt was waiting for her when she returned from the back pasture where she'd had to go to fetch Intrigue. He rested his arms on the top rail and scowled at her horse. "You pull that trick again and you'll be heading for the glue factory," he threatened.

Intrigue snorted and stalked away, unimpressed. Lacy laughed. "I don't think you frighten him. He knows he's the best piece of horseflesh in the county." She made sure the gate was secured and started walking toward the house with her father. "Besides, you can't blame Intrigue. He's as sick of being cooped up here as I am."

"There's no reason for that anymore."

Lacy stopped and squinted through the brilliant sunlight at him. "There isn't?"

"Nope. Dwight called this morning. There hasn't been hide nor hair of any rustlers in the area other than the one you saw. He figures that they must have cleared out."

"No one cleared out," Lacy objected. "I saw a ghost—and he disappeared. Remember?"

Walt gave her a hard look. "Whoever he was, he's gone. But that doesn't mean we shouldn't still take care."

"Right," Lacy muttered. She followed her father inside, then went to wash her hands in the bathroom. What she needed was a good hard ride so she could clear all thoughts of Morgan out of her brain. She wandered into the kitchen in search of food. "I'm going to take Intrigue out for a while this afternoon," she enthused to her mother. "He has to get out and so do I. I think we've both got cabin fever."

Rita nodded. "That's exactly what people were saying last night." She started pulling sandwich fixings out of the fridge. "You really should have been there, Lacy. All anyone wanted to talk about was your ghost."

"In that case, I'm glad I wasn't there," Lacy grumbled. "I don't feel like listening to anyone else laugh about it."

"No one was laughing. They were all a little envious, I think—especially the women. Mabel Edwards kept going on and on about how she wished it was her who'd seen the ghost."

Lacy had to smile at that. "It's a good thing she didn't. She would have fainted dead away."

"Lacy!"

"She would, Mom. Remember that time she found a squirrel in her kitchen. She passed out cold. It took poor Harry an hour to wake her up, then another two to calm her down. If she'd seen my ghost, she'd still be out!''

Rita laughed. ''You've got a good point. Oh, and speaking of ghosts, I asked everyone if they'd heard of Jake Malone.''

Lacy stopped buttering bread at the mention of Jake's name. ''Had they?''

''No, but a few people had heard stories about Sarah Larkspur. She was quite something back then. She ran her ranch all by herself. I guess that was pretty unusual.''

''The way everyone acts is pretty unusual now,'' Lacy murmured.

''Pardon me?''

''Nothing.'' Lacy finished making her sandwich and carted it over to the table to eat.

Rita sat down across from her and folded her arms on the top of the table. ''How about you? Did you ask Cal about it?''

''Uh-huh. But he wasn't much help.'' Lacy scowled as she thought about Cal's attitude. ''He didn't know anything—but he did tell me that the former Larkspur land belongs to him now.'' She chewed on a mouthful of bread and ham. ''If that's the case, I'd sure like to know what Jake was doing on our property.''

''I guess you never know with a ghost,'' Rita said under her breath. She cleared her throat. ''How did things go at Morgan's place?''

Lacy didn't want to talk about Morgan. She'd refused to allow herself to even think about him. Every time she did, she thought about what had almost happened in his bedroom. The whole thing was embarrassing. She'd pretty much attacked him!

That was no way to prove to anyone that she wasn't going to marry him. "Just fine," she lied.

"Did you check out that fridge of his?"

"Mmm-hmm." Lacy munched on her sandwich. "You were right about that fridge. He does need a new one. Oh, and did you know that he doesn't have a dishwasher?"

"Doesn't he?" Rita furrowed her brow while she considered it. "Come to think of it, I guess he doesn't."

"Can you imagine? I don't know how he's survived all these years without one. Oh, and you should have just seen the curtains in the bedrooms, Mother. His sister-in-law hasn't gotten around to changing them, and they desperately need to be changed. They were horrible. Judging by the shape they were in, they must have been hanging there for ages."

Rita's eyebrows rose. "*You* looked at the curtains?"

It was either that or the bed, and she was not going to think about the bed. "Yes, I did, which just goes to show how awful they are." She rolled her eyes. "And when I told Morgan that, he didn't seem to have a clue what I was talking about."

Rita laughed. "It's a man thing, Lacy. I think they're missing the 'curtain' section of their brain."

Lacy finished her sandwich and washed down the last bite with a swallow of milk. "They must be missing the fridge section, too. I don't know how anyone can cope with such a minuscule fridge. Morgan said it was big enough for him, but I don't see how it could be big enough for anybody." She caught sight of the odd smile creeping across her mother's face and paused. "What?"

"Nothing." Rita smiled. "Just that you've said Morgan's name a couple of dozen times in the past five minutes."

Lacy started to utter a denial, then did a quick mental count and winced. "I've just been talking about him, that's all. And...and it doesn't mean—"

Rita held up a hand. "I know. It doesn't mean anything."

"That's right. It doesn't!" Lacy snatched up her hat and stomped out of the house. This thing with Morgan was getting out of hand. Instead of discouraging him, she seemed to be encouraging herself. An image rose in her mind—an image of herself clutching Morgan while his tanned hand moved across her bare breast. Her body throbbed, her breasts tightened, and Lacy softly moaned. What had she been thinking? And what was she going to be thinking next time they were alone together? She needed another solution to her problem, and quickly, or she was going to end up married to Morgan, baking oatmeal cookies and inserting his name into every second sentence.

Unfortunately, she couldn't think of one.

"It's too bad Jake Malone is a ghost," she complained to Oscar as she carted Intrigue's saddle out to the corral. "If he wasn't, maybe he would help." She tossed the saddle over a railing and then climbed over it herself. "If he has to be a ghost, why couldn't he be carrying an armload of cash? Of course, how do I know he wasn't?"

She closed her eyes and pictured him as she'd first seen him—standing in front of the trees. He wasn't carrying any money, but he had been carrying something.

She opened her eyes. "He had a saddlebag, Oscar."

Oscar scooted under the fence and sat down beside her.

"Think of it," Lacy encouraged. "A saddlebag." Her gaze lit on her own saddle, perched on the fence. "If a gunslinger had money, wouldn't he keep it in his saddlebag? I think he just might."

Her heart gave a hopeful leap. Hadn't Janice told her that a ghost carrying money meant he wanted to share a fortune with her? Maybe that's what Jake was doing here. Perhaps he knew of a secret fortune hidden away back there.

That seemed pretty far-fetched. On the other hand, he had led her off into those trees. He could have been trying to tell her that there was something valuable on her land—something that could help her.

"You are definitely losing your marbles," she told herself. Still, it wouldn't hurt to take a look.

AFTER SPENDING ALL NIGHT and a good portion of the day puzzling over Lacy's odd behavior, Morgan finally gave in and consulted the only woman expert he felt comfortable talking to—his brother, Wade.

"Then she just took off," he explained over the phone. "I don't know what came over her." He was sitting in the small room he used as an office, with his booted feet crossed up on the desk, the receiver sandwiched between his shoulder and his ear. "One minute, things were fine. Then she lit out of here as if someone had spooked the bejesus out of her."

Wade's voice rumbled down the phone line, sounding thoughtful as well as a touch patronizing. "Someone probably did."

"How's that?"

"You, Morgan. You probably scared her."

That didn't make a hell of a lot of sense. "What?"

Wade chuckled wisely. "It's a woman thing. They want you to be interested in them, but when you are, they get all riled up about it. The first time I told Cassie I was personally interested in her, she looked terrified."

Morgan choked back a snort. He'd seen Wade dressed in his navy gear, with an arsenal of nasty-looking weapons strapped to his body. If he'd been wearing that outfit when he'd had that conversation with Cassie, well, it was no wonder the poor thing had been frightened.

"I never did figure out what that was all about," Wade ruminated. "Although I suspect it has something to do with sex."

"Sex?" Morgan echoed, startled. He wasn't sure he wanted to have a birds-and-bees discussion with his brother. "What about it?"

"It's the way their minds work. It isn't that they don't want to do it. They just need a little time to get used to the idea of doing it with you. They don't like to be rushed."

Is that what he'd been doing? Rushing her? He hadn't meant for that to happen. It just had—and Lacy had seemed to be enjoying it, too. He thought about her flushed face, the sheen on her lips from his kisses, the feel of her bare breast in his palm, and started to sweat.

"My guess is you came on too strong," Wade continued. "You did say you were in the bedroom, didn't you?"

"Uh-huh." They'd been in the bedroom all right, with his bed temptingly close. Now his jeans were really too tight.

"Well, Lacy probably thought you wanted to get her into bed."

"Of course I wanted to get her into bed." She'd known that, though. If she hadn't figured it out after that kiss they'd shared, she wasn't as bright as he gave her credit for. And she'd been climbing his frame, too. She'd wanted the same thing to happen. "We're talking about getting married. Surely to God she realizes that involves getting into bed sooner or later."

Wade assumed a tone of knowledgeable authority. "You can't assume that with women. They see things a lot differently than we do. What you need to do now is back off. Give Lacy some time to get used to the idea."

"How much time?"

"As much as it takes."

Was Wade measuring time in days or hours—or, God forbid, months? "How much did you give Cassie?"

Wade chuckled. "Not a whole hell of a lot. But that was a different thing. With a woman like Cassie, you can't give her too much time to think. You never know what she'll come up with if you do. But Lacy, now she's a different sort. More levelheaded. After a few days, she'll come around."

"Maybe. You don't know Lacy," Morgan said grimly. He exchanged a few more pleasantries with his brother and hung up the phone. He hadn't been thinking about the physical side of marriage when he decided to propose, but now it seemed to be the only thing he could think about. However, he couldn't honestly fault Lacy. She wasn't the sort of woman to fall into bed with a man just because it felt good. That wasn't a bad quality. As soon as she fell in love with him, she'd probably be a lot more willing.

He just hoped it wouldn't take her too long to do it—or he might not be sane enough to enjoy it.

"ALL RIGHT, WE'RE HERE," Walt announced unnecessarily.

He dismounted from his horse, frowning. "Now, would you mind telling me what in blazes we're doing?"

"I just wanted to take a look around." Lacy swung herself off Intrigue, then held the reins loosely in her hand while studying their position. They were on top of a small rise, with the creek below them, miles of green, rolling countryside in front of them, and to their right, a small grove of trees. "This is it," she said almost to herself. "This is exactly where I was when I spotted Jake's ghost."

Walt muttered something under his breath. "You mean this is where you were when you first spotted that rustler."

Lacy ignored that. "Then he turned and wandered off into those trees—almost as if he wanted me to follow him."

"What in tarnation...?" Walt started. His voice trailed off as Lacy wrapped Intrigue's reins around a fence post. "What are you up to now?"

Lacy flashed a smile. "Just doing a little ghost hunting, Dad."

"Christ!" Walt grabbed his horse's reins and secured them to the post, as well. "I can't believe I'm doing this."

Lacy gave an enormous sigh. Her father had been complaining ever since they'd left the ranch. He thought this was a waste of time and was determined to make sure she knew it. "You didn't have to come along, you know."

"I wasn't about to let you come out here alone."

Lacy rolled her eyes but said nothing. Her father had come close to apoplexy when he'd discovered what she'd had in mind. However, this time, she refused to listen to his "There's no way you're going out there" comment. He'd finally given up and announced he'd accompany her—and Lacy had finally given in and agreed.

"There's nothing out here to worry about," Lacy insisted. "Dwight said no one had spotted any rustlers around here. If that fellow was one, he'd be long gone by now. And if he was a ghost—well, he didn't hurt me last time. I don't see why he'd do it now."

"You never know," Walt muttered.

She started toward the trees. There might not be anything out here to worry about, but she was glad her father was with her. Ghost hunting was kind of spooky.

She led the way with Walt close behind her. "I followed him through here. I think I even called out to him once, but he kept on going." They cleared the trees. Lacy stopped on the other side of the grove.

"When I got here, he was standing over there—beside that rock."

Walt sighed heavily. "I know. Morgan and I checked this spot out just the other morning. We found a set of tracks right where you're pointing."

"Let's see." Lacy hurried over to where she'd last seen Jake's ghost. There were several sets of tracks now, but that was only to be expected. She wasn't interested in tracks anyway. She wanted to know what Jake could have been trying to tell her.

What could it have been? There was nothing unusual in the rocks—they were just a small outcropping, similar to others in the area. Perhaps there was something a little farther along. She took a couple of steps forward.

Then she froze as an unfamiliar, explosive sound reverberated from some bushes to her right. Lacy whirled in that direction. "What was that?"

There was no answer from behind her. Lacy turned. Her father was sitting on the ground, his right hand clutching his left shoulder. Lacy raced over and crouched down beside him.

"Dad! Are you all right?"

"Uh-huh."

"What happened? What...?"

"Well..." Walt gave his head a brief side-to-side shake. Then he pulled his hand away from his arm. Lacy stared at his palm in horrified disbelief. It was covered with blood. "I'm just guessing, of course," Walt said grimly, "but it looks to me as if someone's shooting at us."

WALT WAS IN BED when Morgan arrived at the hospital.

He was sitting upright, with a blue hospital gown tied around his neck and an intravenous line connected to his arm. His face was whiter than usual, the lines around his mouth a little deeper, but on the whole, he looked surprisingly spry for a man who'd just had a bullet dug out of his arm. "I'm just fine," he grumbled when Morgan asked how he was doing. "There's no reason for me to even be in the hospital, much less spending the night here."

Rita reached over from her seat in an orange vinyl chair beside the bed and patted Walt's hand. "They're just keeping you here for observation. It's only for a couple of days. After all, your heart—"

"My heart is fine," Walt growled. He closed his eyes for a brief moment, and Morgan decided the doctor was wise to keep him here for a while.

He stood with his back against the wall, his hat in his hand, feeling as if he'd just walked into a movie. People in his world didn't get shot at very often. As a matter of fact, the only person he knew who'd ever taken a bullet was his brother—and that was only to be expected in his line of work.

He didn't have a clue what had happened. Rita had called him from the hospital, but all she'd told him was that Walt had been shot. As Morgan took in her worn, worried face, he wished whoever had pulled that trigger was in this room, as well. He wasn't a violent man, but right now, he'd enjoy showing the fellow behind this shooting the error of his ways.

He crossed the room to settle into a chair on the other side of the bed. "Do either of you two feel up to filling me in?"

Walt grimaced. "It was my own darn fault, I suppose. Lacy was bound and determined she was going to take a ride out to the southeast pasture—right around the area where she'd spotted that rustler the other day. I told her to forget it, but she was all het up about it. I finally gave in and told her that if she was going, I'd ride along with her."

Morgan stiffened at that. "Lacy? You mean Lacy was there, too?"

"Uh-huh." Walt nodded in the direction of the door. "She's out there now, telling the sheriff all about it."

Morgan could actually feel his blood pressure rise. He hadn't seen hide nor hair of Lacy since his arrival a few minutes ago. He'd vaguely assumed she was off getting coffee or something of that nature, and he'd been too concerned about Walt to ask. "She wasn't shot, too, was she?"

"No, no. She's fine." He beamed proudly. "She's got a lot of guts, that girl. Had me on my horse and hightailing it out of there before you could even say jack rabbit."

"Did she?" Morgan wasn't as impressed as Walt. He was fighting a sudden dizziness brought on by the very idea of someone firing a gun at Lacy. What in hell had gotten into her? They'd told her to stay close to home, damn it! Had she done that? No! She'd gotten some fool urge to take a ride out to the very place where she'd seen that rustler—and gotten herself shot at in the process. Ever since she'd seen that so-called ghost, she'd been acting peculiar. She'd even been talking about curtains yesterday! Christ, the next thing he knew, she'd be telling what color looked good on him, too.

Rita looked across the bed at him. "I'm going to

stay in town tonight so I can keep an eye on Walt. Will you see that Lacy gets home safely?''

"Yes, ma'am," Morgan lied. He'd see that Lacy got home. He wasn't sure about the safely part. The way he was feeling right now, he couldn't guarantee anything except that Lacy was never, *ever*, going to pull a harebrained stunt like that again. She might not live through it, and he didn't think he would, either.

He was busy formulating his lecture, which started with "What in tarnation did you think you were doing?" and ended along the same lines when the door opened and Lacy stepped into the room. Her face was the color of old snow, her freckles standing out in sharp relief. The eyes that met his were wide and shocked-looking, and her lower lip trembled. "Morgan!" she exclaimed. Then she was across the room, in his arms, hugging him fiercely. "I'm so glad you're here."

Morgan's chest constricted, and his annoyance with her vanished as relief seeped through him. She was here. She was safe. He could always tell her off later. Right now, he just wanted to take care of her. He hugged her back. "Are you okay?" he asked into her hair.

"I'm fine." Lacy's voice was muffled against his chest. She raised her head so he could see her face and managed a small smile. "I'm just a little shook up, that's all." She glanced toward her parents, flushed, then moved out of his arms. "How about you, Dad? How are you doing?"

Morgan waited while Walt assured her that he was fine and went into another tirade about why he shouldn't be in a hospital. Rita explained the arrangements to Lacy. "Walt's staying here and that's that. I'm going to stay with Doris and Henry. Morgan's going to take you home, Lacy."

Lacy's gaze flew to his face, while her own colored. "Maybe I should stay with you, Mom."

"There's no need for that." Rita patted her shoulder. "Your father's going to be fine and so am I. But you've got to get some sleep. Go on home and I'll talk to you in the morning."

Lacy still hesitated. "You're sure?"

"She's sure," Morgan cut in. He slid an arm around her shoulders. "Come on, honey. I'll take you home."

Lacy looked at him for a second, then nodded. "All right." She kissed her father's cheek, gave her mother a hug and accompanied Morgan out of the room. "Mother shouldn't have bothered you," she said as they walked toward the front entrance. "I could have found another ride."

"It's no bother, Lacy." He gave her a sharp glance as he opened the door. "Maybe you should be spending the night in the hospital, as well. You don't look too good."

"I'm okay." She took a deep breath of cool night air and managed a smile. "It's just something of a shock, that's all."

"You're not the only one," Morgan mumbled under his breath. He was feeling pretty shook up himself, and no one had taken a shot at him.

Lacy was silent as they got into his truck. Morgan watched her fasten her seat belt with hands that trembled slightly, then switched on the ignition and drove out of the parking lot. He kept checking on her out of the corner of his eye as he drove past the town and into the countryside. She was just sitting there, biting down on her bottom lip.

Morgan stretched out a hand to give her shoulder a pat. "The doctor said your dad is going to be fine, honey."

"I know." Some of the tension went out of her at his touch. "But he shouldn't be there at all. This is really my fault, Morgan. I never should have let Dad come along with me."

"It's not your fault. Walt's a grown man. He can make his own decisions." Morgan slowed for a curve. "Besides, if it's anyone's fault, it's mine."

"Yours? How can it be your fault? You weren't even there!"

"That's not the point." Scowling, Morgan peered through the windshield at the ribbon of road revealed by his headlights. "I should have put an end to this ghost nonsense when you first started talking about it."

Lacy's voice hardened. "Oh, you should have, should you?"

"You're darn right I should have!" Morgan could have given himself a good swift kick for not doing that. It was Wade's fault, of course. Why in hell had he listened to his brother? He'd never done that before. "This just goes to show how much you need a man around, Lacy."

"It does, does it?"

"Uh-huh." Morgan took a quick, sideways look at her. "Oh, I'm not blaming you. It's probably those hormones of yours acting up that makes you behave like this."

"Hormones?" Lacy's voice rose. "You think hormones are the reason I saw a ghost?"

"No. I think hormones are the reason you think you saw a ghost." He stopped the truck in her yard and shifted to face her. "After we're married, these sorts of things won't be happening. I'll see to that."

"You will, will you?" Lacy smiled sweetly. "How are you going to do that? Have them surgically removed after the wedding?"

Morgan chuckled. "I don't reckon you can do that, honey. It's just something a man has to learn to live with. But what I can do is make sure that when you're having an attack of 'em, you don't go off and do something stupid."

Lacy's lips thinned to an ominous line. "You can, can you?"

"Uh-huh."

Lacy settled back in her seat with a flounce. "Up yours," she muttered.

"What was that?"

"You know exactly what I said and I meant it, too! I don't need you or any other man telling me how to behave!"

Morgan started to open his door. "If the way you acted today is any indication, I'd say you do."

Her eyes flashed irritation. "How did I act today?"

Morgan knew the exact word to describe it. "Irrationally," he shot back. "You acted irrationally and you know it."

"Irrationally?" Lacy's voice lowered to a dangerous pitch. "Just what did I do that was so irrational? Take a ride on my horse?"

It occurred to Morgan that he was losing control of this conversation. "There wasn't anything irrational about that. It was where you rode your horse that was irrational. A few days ago, you caught sight of a rustler. It doesn't take a whole lot of brains to realize that riding into a place where you've seen a rustler isn't a smart move."

"And it doesn't take a whole lot of brains for a rustler to realize that if he's been spotted, he should get out of there!" Lacy countered. "Besides, it wasn't a rustler I saw. It was a ghost! Ghosts don't rustle cattle, Morgan! They've got better things to do with their time."

"Now, Lacy—"

"Even if it was a rustler, it was a stupid one," Lacy went on furiously. "There's no reason for a rustler to hang around there. It's a lousy place to hold cattle, it's not close to any decent transportation, and he doesn't seem to have been taking anybody's cattle anyway!"

A slow chill meandered its way up Morgan's spine. She was right. No one had reported any missing cattle. And a rustler who hung around after he'd been spotted wouldn't last long in that profession.

"Furthermore, there is nothing wrong with my hormones!" Lacy continued. "I took a ride with my father and some creep shot at us. What that has to do with hormones is beyond me!" She shoved the door open and jumped out. "Thanks for the ride. Don't bother coming in! You never know when I might get a hormone attack and do something irrational!"

"That's for sure," Morgan growled.

Lacy made an inarticulate sound of anger and slammed the door so hard the entire truck rattled. Morgan watched her storm into the house while he struggled with his own temper and debated the wisdom of going after her and finishing this conversation. The lights came on inside, and he had a feeling he wasn't invited.

He slammed the truck into gear and swung around in the driveway. Damn, he was sick of dealing with women. What in hell had possessed Lacy to turn into one?

9

"WHAT IN BLAZES IS GOING on out there?" Wade bellowed.

Morgan flinched at the sound and yanked the receiver away from his ear. He wasn't in a great mood this morning anyway. Having the goldarn phone ring at six in the morning hadn't done anything to improve it—and hearing Wade shout at him wasn't helping the situation. "If that's your new way of announcing yourself on the phone, Wade, I've got to tell you, it's not much of an improvement," he snarled back.

"I want to know what's going on!"

Morgan took a long gulp of strong black coffee from the mug in his hand and squinted around the room. "Let's see. It's morning out here, Wade, in case you've forgotten. Early morning. The sun's just getting up and so am I. I'm drinking a cup of coffee and eating a piece of toast. Apart from that—"

Wade's low growl alerted him that this wasn't the right answer. "That's not what I'm talking about. I'm talking about the shooting out there last night."

Morgan slowly uncurled his spine. "How do you know about that?"

Wade's sigh was huge and impatient. "For God's sake, Morgan, I'm in Naval Intelligence! What do you think we do all day?"

"I've got no idea," Morgan grumbled back at him. "But I always figured it had more to do with water than it did cattle rustlers."

"It does, but in this case it doesn't. Now, how about filling me in?"

Morgan didn't feel much like going into it again, but there was no point in arguing with Wade. He'd always been hard to deal with in the morning. He stretched out an arm, hauled over a chair and settled into it while he told Wade the whole story. "I don't know what got into Lacy," he concluded. "She's usually a levelheaded woman, but this ghost thing has really gotten to her. It must be those hormones you were telling me about."

There was silence—followed by Wade's voice, deep and thoughtful. "I'm not so sure about that," he said.

Morgan was so surprised he almost dropped the phone. "What's that you said?"

"I'm not so sure. You can never tell with a woman. Sometimes when it seems they're dead wrong about something, it turns out that they're right on the mark."

He sounded perfectly serious. "Are you telling me you believe this ghost story of Lacy's?" Morgan demanded.

Wade hesitated. "I'm not discounting it."

"Well, hell," Morgan exclaimed, exasperated. "It wasn't a ghost that shot Walt. I know that for a fact."

"I'm not suggesting it was a ghost. But I've got my doubts about this rustler theory, as well."

"Then who do you think did it?"

"I have no idea," Wade admitted. "But I don't

want you going anywhere near that place, Morgan. Not until I've had some time to think about this."

"Wade—"

"You're my only brother," Wade said gruffly. "I don't want anything happening to you." Before Morgan could remind him that he was the one in the military and thus the one running a greater risk with his life, Wade had hung up.

Morgan stared at the receiver for a moment, then returned it to its cradle. Before Wade had married, Morgan wasn't sure he often remembered that he had a brother, much less worried about something happening to him. His concern was touching—but also a little disconcerting. So were Wade's other comments. It made Morgan wonder about him all over again. It must come from being around water all the time—and from being married to Cassie. She'd done something to his brain. Morgan sure hoped that didn't happen to him after he got married.

If he got married. He went over to the sink and washed his few dishes while he reviewed the situation. Lacy was proving to be a lot more difficult than he'd anticipated. Maybe he should consider calling this whole marriage idea off. She still wasn't sold on it herself.

And that was just too bad. He opened a cupboard door and shoved in a plate. He thought again about how she'd felt in his arms, about the life he'd planned here, with her, and pushed that notion aside never to be thought of again. Lacy might not be sold on the idea, but he was. He wanted that more than he'd wanted anything in his life and he was determined to make it happen. As soon as she got over this ghost nonsense she'd be back to her normal, sensible self.

If it *was* nonsense.

"Christ," Morgan muttered, irritated. "Now I'm getting as bad as Lacy and Wade."

He banged a cupboard door closed and stomped outside to find Eddie. There was nothing like a conversation with a regular rancher type to put a man's feet on the ground.

Eddie was as astonished by the whole business as Morgan had been.

"Shot?" he exclaimed when Morgan told him about the incident. His eyes rounded to the shape of the full moon. "Someone took a shot at Walt Johnson."

"That's right." After a night of thinking about it, Morgan could still hardly believe it himself. "I figured I should tell you. I don't want you or any of the hands riding out alone. And make darn sure you've got a rifle with you at all times."

"You got it!"

"Make sure the hands know, Eddie." Morgan started to turn away, then had another thought. "Oh, and you might want to keep Susan around home for the next while—until the sheriff finds that character or we're positive he's gone."

"I'll tell her." Eddie made a face. "But knowing her, she'll want to ride out there and take a look for herself."

Morgan gave him a quizzical look. "She will?"

"She might. You can never tell with Susan." He lowered his voice. "And I'll you something else, Morgan. Me telling her not to is a good way to make her want to get out there."

This sounded familiar. "Is that so?"

"Yup. Now if I *ask* her not to, she might just go along with it."

Morgan squinted against the early-morning sun. "You mean if you tell her, she won't do it, but if you ask her, she will?"

"That's about the size of it." Eddie looked as puzzled by this as Morgan felt. "It's something about women. You tell me not to go, I think, well, he's a pretty smart fellow. If he doesn't think it's a good idea, it probably isn't. Women don't look at it that way. You tell them they got to stay close to home and they think 'To hell with you, buster,' serve you something called tuna surprise and go do it anyway."

Morgan shuddered in sympathy. He wasn't fond of fish himself. "Is that so?"

"That's how it seems to me. But say something like, 'Honey, I'm just worried sick that something will happen to you and I just couldn't live with myself if it did. It'll do my mind a pile of good if I can count on you staying around here so you'll be safe.' Well, they'll grill you a steak, bake an apple pie and stay in the bedroom, waiting for you to get home." He leered. "And it won't be pie that's on their minds, either."

Morgan scratched the back of his head while he considered this. "That doesn't make much sense."

"Tell me about it." Eddie worked in silence for a few minutes. "You know what else doesn't make a lot of sense, Morgan? Those rustlers."

"How's that?"

"It just seems mighty dumb to me. Not that I know the first thing about rustling cattle, but if I was

going to do it, I wouldn't hide in that area. I'd pick a
place near a road, where I could park my truck without being seen. And if someone spotted me, I'd
hightail it out of there. I wouldn't hang around to
see if they came back."

"Good point," Morgan conceded.

"Besides, I thought the sheriff had taken a good
look around there and hadn't seen hide nor hair of
anyone."

"There's a lot of bush back there, Eddie. Easy for a
man to stay out of sight."

"I suppose," Eddie agreed but didn't look convinced.

Morgan wasn't convinced, either. The more he
thought about it, the more improbable this rustler
theory seemed.

"HONESTLY, OSCAR, DO YOU have to be underfoot all
the time?" Lacy complained. Oscar gave her a re-
proachful look and slunk across the yard. Lacy
winced as she watched him go. "I'm sorry," she
called after him.

Oscar looked at her over his shoulder, gave her a
disdainful glare and left. In the past hour, she'd
yelled at Oscar, threatened the cat and even called
Intrigue a bad name. And it was only eight o'clock.

By the time evening came around, she'd probably
have antagonized every animal on the ranch.

She checked on the calves and went into the barn
to clean up after the horses. She knew what was
wrong with her. She hadn't had enough sleep. As a
matter of fact, she'd hardly had any sleep. When she
wasn't berating herself for being responsible for her
father's injury, she'd been imagining she heard

noises, and when she wasn't doing that, she'd been thinking about Morgan.

She hadn't been very nice to him. All right, she admitted reluctantly, she'd been downright rude. He'd dropped everything to come racing into town to help them out, and she'd yelled at him. Granted, he was an opinionated chauvinist with ideas about women long out of style, but that was beside the point. He'd always been like that and she hadn't yelled at him about it.

Of course, she hadn't been contemplating marrying him then, either.

She paused in the midst of her chores to lean against the railing. It was beginning to appear as if she didn't have a whole lot of choices here. It didn't even seem that her ghost had been a ghost. Ghosts did not shoot at people. Maybe he had been a rustler. After all, a ghost wouldn't shoot real bullets.

So her hope of salvation was slim at best. She was going to lose this ranch—or she was going to have to marry Morgan.

Maybe she should just give in and agree to do it. It might not be so bad. He didn't seem to expect her to cook and clean—at least that's what he was saying now. Then again, what about those descendants he was so het up on getting. Who would take care of them? She pictured the bedrooms, redecorated with children's colors. Her mind took another tour, down the hall, on into the master bedroom at the back. There would be some heavy-duty activity going on in there if they wanted to get those descendants.

The prospect wasn't displeasing.

Lacy gave her head a shake. What was the matter with her? Every time she thought about Morgan, she thought about attacking him. Maybe she did have some kind of hormone problem!

She finished up in the barn and was headed for the house, intending to give her mother another call, when a black truck turned off the main road and bumped down the gravel road toward her. A black truck. Morgan's black truck. The same truck she'd stomped out of last night.

Stopping in her tracks, Lacy watched it approach. She didn't feel like facing Morgan or anyone else this morning, but it had to be done. At the very least, she owed him an apology for yelling at him. Granted, he'd deserved it, but he'd also gone out of his way to give her a hand. Besides, he'd been right. Riding out there had been a dumb thing to do.

This was a good opportunity to get it over with.

It was also a good opportunity to prove to herself that she could act cool and collected around him.

He opened the door and climbed out of his truck—a tall, masculine-looking figure dressed in his customary black jeans and shirt. "Morning, Lacy."

Lacy took one look at his sinewy forearms, the strong column of his throat, his glittering blue eyes, and realized that not being affected by Morgan was going to be a difficult task. "Hi, Morgan." She ordered her feet to move and they did, taking her in his direction. She stopped a couple of feet away from him, squinting in the sunlight.

His eyes searched her face. "How are you feeling this morning? Did you get any sleep?"

"Some," Lacy lied.

"You still look a mite pale." He gestured toward

the house with his chin. "Can we go inside? I'd like to have a word with you."

Lacy didn't move. Morgan's voice had grim overtones, and there was an equally grim look in his eye. He must want to finish the argument they'd started yesterday. Lacy didn't feel up to it. Right now, if he started in on her, she'd either lock herself in her bedroom or burst into tears.

She drew in a breath and raised her head to look him square in the eye. "If it's about last night, I, uh, do feel I owe you an apology."

Morgan looked completely at sea. "An apology?"

"Yes. I was, um, a little upset yesterday what with Dad getting shot and everything. I shouldn't have taken it out on you."

Morgan grinned and patted her shoulder. "Don't worry about it, Lacy. You'd had a bit of a shock. It's only to be expected that you would act that way— you being a woman and all."

Lacy clenched one hand into a fist. How could she be so madly attracted to him and still want to punch him in the mouth at the same time?

"Besides, I'm not so sure you were wrong," Morgan added thoughtfully.

"What?"

He put an arm around her shoulders and propelled her toward the house. "Let's go inside. The sheriff should be here shortly. We both want to have a talk with you."

AFTER SEEING A GHOST, dealing with Morgan's proposal and accepting the fact that someone had actually shot her father, Lacy figured every outlandish thing that could happen had already happened.

That wasn't the case. Fifteen minutes after Morgan's arrival, she realized another unpredictable thing had happened.

Morgan and the sheriff had lost their ability to think rationally.

She pushed her hair out of her eyes and studied the two men sitting around her mother's kitchen table. Dwight Lanigan's usually bland features were set and narrowed. Morgan had a similar expression, although Lacy couldn't help noticing that he looked good with stern eyes and compressed lips.

"What do you mean you aren't sure it was a rustler who shot at Dad and me? It had to be a rustler. Who else could it be?"

"You never know," Dwight muttered. He exchanged a look with Morgan and Lacy had the urge to bang their heads together. It seemed that recently, whenever she was in a room with two other people, all they did was look at one another every time she spoke. It was getting a little tiresome.

"What do you mean 'You never know'?" Lacy demanded. She glared at the sheriff, then at Morgan. "What harebrained idea have you two come up with now?"

Morgan leaned back in his chair. "It isn't entirely our idea, Lacy. You said pretty much the same thing last night—that it didn't make sense for cattle rustlers to be hanging around up there."

"I know, but you didn't agree."

"Well, I've had a little time to think on it, and I believe you've got a point." He thrust his thumb toward the sheriff. "And when I mentioned it to Dwight here, well, he agreed with me."

Lacy dropped her head back to stare up at the ceil-

ing. Men! When you wanted them to agree with
you, they didn't. When you didn't want them to
agree with you, they did. How did any woman manage to live with one without going around the bend?
"I was upset last night, Morgan. I didn't mean for
you to—"

Dwight cleared his throat. "It's not just that. I've
been concerned about you folks for some time
now."

Lacy swung around to gape at him. "You have?"

"Uh-huh. You've had a lot of problems around
here the past couple of years. More than your fair
share, I'd say."

"I agree, but I don't see what that has to do
with..." She paused. "Just a minute. Surely you
aren't suggesting that those things that happened to
us—that they weren't accidents."

Dwight shrugged a shoulder. "I'm just saying it's
something to consider."

"That's ludicrous!" Lacy looked from one man to
the other, wondering if this was a joke. But there
wasn't one trace of amusement on their faces. "Why
would anyone do things like that to us?"

Morgan shifted uncomfortably in his seat.
"There's always the possibility that someone wants
you to sell out."

"Who? And why?"

"I've got no idea," Dwight admitted. "But as I
said, the matter needs some investigating." He
leaned forward. "How about you? You got any
ideas who might want you off this ranch?"

"*No!*"

"Anyone been around, asking about buying it
up?"

Lacy shook her head. "Only the people from that farm corporation company—and they ask everybody. And Cal did mention that he'd buy the place if we needed him to, but he was just being neighborly. Besides, why would anyone pick on us? Our land isn't any more valuable than anyone else's."

Dwight pursed his lips while he considered that. "I don't know, but after this shooting, I want to look into it."

"How are you going to go about doing that? You won't upset my father, will you? He's—"

"I'm not trying to upset anyone, but I've got a job to do and I mean to do it." He rose. "One more thing. While this is up in the air, I don't want you staying out here on your own."

"Excuse me?"

"You really shouldn't." Dwight looked embarrassed but determined. "Someone did take a shot at you. Until we know for certain who that someone is, you shouldn't be here by yourself."

Too much testosterone, Lacy thought hysterically. The men around here must buy it in bulk. "That's ridiculous. I'm perfectly capable—"

"No one is saying you aren't capable," Morgan interrupted. "We're just concerned about your well-being."

Lacy could have smacked him. "You're in on this, too, are you?"

"You bet your boots I am." Morgan's look brooked no opposition. "I'm not giving someone another opportunity to take a shot at you, and that's that."

"It is, is it?"

"Yes," Morgan said. "It is."

Lacy's glance took in their determined masculine faces. "I can't just leave here. There's tons of work to do...the cattle to check...the horses...and I can't leave the place unattended."

"Dwight and I have already discussed that. I'm going to send Matt over here, and Dwight will have one of his men stay at the ranch, as well."

"And where am I supposed to go? Have you arranged that, too?"

"Yup," Morgan said, grinning smugly. "You can stay with me. We can come over here from time to time to make sure things are under control. Or, if you don't want to do that, you can go stay with someone else. I'm sure Janice Delany would be pleased to put you up. Or your aunt. But you're not staying here."

"You can't—"

"Maybe I can't," Morgan interrupted in a silky smooth tone. "But your folks can."

His expression was that of someone who'd just played the winning hand in a poker game. He had, too. Lacy would do anything to keep them from worrying. She slumped her shoulders in defeat. "I don't have much choice in this, do I?"

"Nope," Morgan said.

Lacy turned to Dwight, hoping for assistance. He looked apologetic, but stood firm. "Sorry, Lacy. I'm afraid I have to agree with Morgan on this one."

Lacy gave up. There was no way these two were going to leave without her. "Oh, all right," she said ungraciously. "I guess I'll stay with Morgan."

She stomped out of the room to put together a few things. Overprotective men! One of these days they were going to drive her crazy!

WADE HADN'T SAID ANYTHING to Morgan about a woman's reaction to being forced out of her own home. However, by the time they'd arrived at his place, Morgan had figured it out for himself.

They didn't look on it too kindly.

Right now, Morgan didn't care—and he wasn't about to apologize for it, either. Dwight might be out to lunch about this, but Morgan was in no mood to take any chances. Someone had shot at Walt and Lacy. Walt was safe in the hospital. Lacy was going to be safe in his house, and if she didn't like it, well, that was too bad.

He just wished she wouldn't make such an effort to ensure that he didn't like it.

He carried her single bag up the stairs and dumped it into the first room he came to. He grinned when he realized it was the one with the ugly curtains. Good. Maybe that would give her something to think about rather than how ticked off she was at him.

Lacy was in the living room when he went back down. She gave him a cold, tight-lipped smile when he entered the room. "Well, here I am," she said. "I hope you're happy."

"Thrilled to bits," Morgan muttered as he took in her resentful expression. "There's nothing I like better than having a houseguest who isn't speaking to me."

Lacy's cheeks flared red. "I suppose you think I'm being a real bitch about this?"

"I think you're giving it one hell of a try." Morgan held up a hand. "Not that I blame you. I wouldn't like being dragged out of my house, either. But I didn't see that I had much choice."

Lacy's eyes flashed. "Of course you did. You could have told Dwight he was crazy and—"

"I couldn't do that. There's a chance he isn't crazy at all. Granted, it's a small chance, but I'm not willing to take it." He lowered his voice. "You folks have been real good to me, Lacy. I'm not about to stand by and let something happen to you. And if that makes you mad at me, well, you'll just have to be mad at me."

"I'm not mad at you." She sat down. "It's—it's just a little upsetting, that's all. First Dad getting shot and then Dwight suggesting—you know, what he was suggesting. It's hard to believe this is all happening."

"I'm sure it is."

"I didn't mean to take it out on you. You're trying to do the right thing, I suppose, and I guess I should be grateful."

"It's no hardship having you here, Lacy."

For an instant their gazes met. Lacy flushed again and looked away. "Now what? I'm here. What am I going to do all day? Cook and clean?"

Visions of tuna surprise rose in Morgan's mind. "You can do that, I reckon if you have a mind to. There's no need, though. The place is clean enough, and I'll throw on a couple of steaks later." He had a sudden inspiration. "I was thinking that you might consider giving Eddie a hand. He's checking for foot rot, but he's not very good at it. He could use a little advice."

"Oh." Lacy's expression softened. "Well, I suppose since I'm here I might as well do that." Morgan could tell she was pleased with the idea. "What about you? What are you...?"

There was nothing Morgan would have liked better than to spend the rest of the day with her. However, she was still in a bit of a snit. Wade's advice had covered that. "When a woman gets in a mood, it's best to make yourself scarce. If you're lucky, she'll forget all about it by the time you get back." "I've got a couple of errands to run. And I'd like to have a word with Cal."

"Cal? Why?"

Morgan grinned and gave her a swift kiss on the cheek. "I'd like to know a little more about this gunslinger of yours."

CAL WAS NOWHERE IN SIGHT when Morgan turned into his driveway. He pulled to a stop in front of the house and climbed out, shaking his head as he noted the faded white paint on the outbuildings and the loose shingles on Cal's narrow bungalow. It made his suspicions almost seem absurd. Cal's luck hadn't been much better than the Johnsons—and there were no suggestions that anyone was trying to force him off his land.

Fifteen minutes later, his suspicions seemed even more absurd. He sat in Cal's living room, making stilted conversation, while trying to figure out the best way to bring up the subject of Lacy's ghost.

Thankfully, Cal made it easy for him. After they'd exhausted the topic of the weather and the possibility of rustlers, Cal cleared his throat. "You look like a man with something on his mind, Morgan."

Morgan nodded. "I am. I wanted to ask you about Jake Malone."

"Jake Malone?" Cal chuckled. "His ghost isn't hanging around your place now, is it?"

"Not that I've seen, no. And it's not really Jake Malone I'm interested in anyway. It's that relative of yours—the one who got killed in that gunfight."

"Mom's great-uncle Karl? Why would you be interested in him?"

"Well, according to Lacy, it's likely that the reason Jake up and shot Karl was because he was making life difficult for Sarah Larkspur. Lacy said he probably wanted to drive her off her ranch."

"Maybe he did. Who knows? It was a long time ago. Things were different then. Neighbors didn't always get along."

"True enough. But the thing is, Cal, it seems to me that the same sort of stuff is going on now."

"How's that?"

"Lacy said Karl and his boys were suspected of doing all kinds of damage to the Larkspurs. Burning her hay. Cutting her fences. That sort of thing—the same things that have been happening to the Johnsons."

"They've had a run of bad luck all right. Surely to God you're not suggesting that there's more to it than that?"

"It just seems mighty strange to me, all those accidents. That's why I came to see you. I thought you might be able to shed some light on the situation."

"Me?" Cal chuckled. "How?"

"Well, this relation of yours—Karl—he must have had some reason for wanting the Larkspurs to get off their land. I thought maybe someone might have the same motive now."

Cal shook his head. "I can't think of one. I don't know why Karl would have wanted to do that in the first place—unless he just wanted to spread out a little more." He shrugged. "I'm not sure those stories are true anyway."

Lacy was right about Cal, Morgan decided. He wasn't the least bit interested in his long-lost relations. "Can you think of anyone who'd want to see the Johnsons forced off their place?"

Cal shook his head. "Not offhand I can't. Walt and Rita are good people, Morgan. But if you're looking for suspects, I'd say I have to top the list. I've offered to buy out Walt more than once." He held up a hand. "That doesn't mean I want him to go. I don't. But I sure don't want one of those corporate fellows coming in here, either—and neither does Walt. If they do end up having to sell, well, I'm willing to take it on."

"You don't have to worry about that. Lacy and I are fixing to get married. She and I will be taking over the place."

Cal's jaw dropped. "You and Lacy are getting married?"

It wasn't entirely settled, but Morgan wasn't about to let Cal know that. "Uh-huh."

"Does Lacy know?"

"Of course Lacy knows," Morgan said, irritated. "When did you think I was going to break it to her? When we arrived at the church?"

"No, of course not." Cal fingered his jaw. "It's just something of a surprise, that's all. And Lacy never mentioned it the other day when she was here. As a matter of fact, she said very clearly that she wasn't ever getting married."

She had, had she? Well, she was wrong about that. "It's just a woman thing," Morgan explained comfortably. He got to his feet, tired of the conversation. "I've got to get going. Thanks for your help, Cal."

"Anytime," Cal muttered. He rose slowly and walked Morgan to the door in contemplative silence. Morgan shook his hand in the hallway and was just stepping outside when Cal spoke again. "That's a pretty interesting way you've got of getting more land. I should try it myself sometime."

Morgan scowled at him. "I'm not marrying Lacy to get her land!"

"No?" Cal's bushy eyebrows rose. "Why are you doing it, then? Surely you aren't going to tell me that you're in love with her?"

Morgan stared at him for a moment, then turned and stomped out. However, as he climbed into his truck, he wondered if that was the real reason he'd come up with the idea in the first place.

10

THERE WAS NOTHING like cattle to put a woman in a good mood, Lacy decided that evening.

A day working with Morgan's heifers had gone a long way toward restoring her equilibrium. The hard work had tired her physically, if not mentally, and had given her something else to think about. Coming back to the house to the smell of steaks grilling, potatoes frying and Morgan whistling tunelessly in the kitchen hadn't been bad, either.

Now, curled up in one corner of the sofa with a cup of coffee in her hand, she felt better than she had since that awful moment when she realized her father had been shot. "You don't really think someone is trying to drive us off our land, do you?" she asked Morgan.

Morgan turned his cup around and around in his palms. "I don't know what to think. Like you said, the whole thing seems mighty suspicious."

She had said that—and he had taken her seriously. Any remnants of annoyance she'd felt about being forced out of her house disappeared. It wasn't his fault he was a man. He was just trying to do the right thing. "You said you were going to talk to Cal. Did you?"

"Uh-huh. You were right. He doesn't know a hell of a lot about it. And he's got no idea why Karl would have wanted the Larkspur place. He suggested that maybe he just plain didn't like them."

"I suppose that's possible," Lacy reflected. "Although it's hard to believe someone would go to all that trouble simply to get rid of someone he didn't like." There was another option. Could it be that she was right—that there was something valuable out there, something her ghostly gunslinger was trying to show her, and Karl had known about it?

"Or maybe he did just want their land."

"Maybe." Lacy chewed on her lip. Tomorrow, come hell or high water, she was going to take her Dad's old shotgun and go back out there to take another look. If Morgan didn't like it—too bad.

She smothered a yawn. She'd deal with that tomorrow. Tonight, she was too tired.

Morgan set down his mug and stood. "You look worn out, Lacy, and I know I am. It's time we hit the hay."

"I suppose." Lacy eyed him warily as she uncurled herself and slid to her feet. They were alone. She was spending the night. He'd put her things in the room with the ugly curtains—the rat—but in the back of her mind she fully expected...

She wasn't sure what she expected, but it didn't happen. Morgan flicked a kiss across her mouth, picked up her empty mug and nodded in the direction of the stairs. "You go on up. I'll take care of these."

"All right." She watched him carry the dishes out of the room, then turned toward the stairs. "Good night, Morgan."

He didn't even turn around. "Night."

Lacy hesitated, then went up the stairs and into

her room. She made a face as she switched on the light. Morgan had given her this room on purpose—probably as a way to get even with her for being so cantankerous when they arrived. She smiled to herself. She really couldn't blame him. She had been in a bad mood.

She tugged off her clothes, pulled on her peach-colored flannel jammies and was just climbing into bed when she heard Morgan's footsteps as he climbed the stairs. Her pulse leaped in anticipation, then settled back as the footsteps clomped past her room without even hesitating.

Lacy switched off her light and lay down. This wasn't what she'd expected to happen. She'd thought that Morgan wanted her to stay at his place so he could take advantage of the situation—but it appeared that she was wrong. She wasn't even sure that Morgan knew there was a situation!

She flounced over onto her side. She should have known better. Morgan wasn't the subtle seduction type. If he wanted to spend the night with a woman, he'd come right out and say so.

He hadn't done that with her.

She closed her eyes and willed herself to go to sleep. It didn't work. She'd been tired before, but she wasn't tired now. She was wide awake. She could still feel the press of Morgan's mouth on her own. When she touched her tongue to her lips, she could taste him. Her breasts ached in fond remembrance of being close against his hard chest, her thighs tingling from the feel of his. She could hear him moving around his room, and the thought of him undressing was the most erotic thought of all.

She sat up and switched on the light. This was

silly. They were both mature adults. She was positive Morgan wanted to sleep with her. He just didn't think it was gentlemanly or something. She wanted to sleep with him, too. That didn't mean she wanted to marry him. She just wanted to stop feeling like this.

She got out of bed. Lots of people had affairs that didn't lead to marriage. There was no reason why she and Morgan couldn't do that. Besides, she wasn't going to be able to sleep tonight knowing he was only footsteps away.

She took a deep breath, slipped on her housecoat and padded down the hall to Morgan's room. The door was open a few inches. Probably, Lacy surmised, so Morgan could ensure her safety. She could see him through the opening, standing at right angles to her, still fully dressed except for an untucked, half-buttoned shirt.

Lacy's heart beat so fast she could feel the blood tearing around her body. She gulped in some air, then cleared her throat. "Morgan?"

Morgan swung around. "Hey, Lacy. Do you need something?"

Just you. "Not really." Her gaze skimmed down his chest, fastened on his belt buckle, then wandered to the bulge below. "I was just, uh, thinking."

"About what?"

"Sex."

"What?"

"I mean, uh, sexual compatibility," Lacy amended. She tottered forward a couple of steps, exerting a tremendous amount of willpower not to jump him then and there. She wanted to rip off his clothes, push him down onto the bed and touch every part of him with every part of her. "If we're going to talk about getting married, we should talk about sexual compatibility."

Morgan's furrowed brow suggested that idea had never crossed his mind. "What about it?"

Honestly, this man! Last time they'd been alone in this room, he'd had his hands all over her. Now it looked like she was going to have to draw him a picture. "We don't know if we are. Sexually compatible, that is."

Morgan chuckled. "You don't have to worry about that, honey. If the other time we were alone here is any indication, I don't think there'll be any problems."

He did remember! Good. If he'd forgotten, she'd have thrown something at him. "I'm not so sure," Lacy said. "We didn't exactly, uh, do very much." Come on, Morgan, do something—fast. "It might be a good idea if we, uh, found out. Beforehand, I mean."

"You mean now?"

"Yes." Right now. This second. Immediately if not sooner. Lacy tried a careless shrug. "It seems like a good time to find out."

Morgan eyed her while he considered. "You sure about that, Lacy? When we tried it before, you got spooked."

"I'm not going to get spooked."

"You're sure?"

"I'm absolutely positive."

"Are you?" He studied her while his eyes darkened and his color rose. Then he nodded. "In that case, I have to say that it sounds like a darn good idea to me."

He peeled off his shirt.

Lacy wasn't sure if he expected her to strip down, as well, or if he even had a thought about how they should proceed, but she wasn't going to wait any longer for him to figure it out. She was going to do everything she'd ever fantasized with his body. She was going to feel it. She was going to put her tongue against it, touch every inch of it, stroke her palms along it, check out those thigh muscles...and every other muscle he had. Then maybe this stupid, juvenile, hormonal reaction would be over and done with.

She took an eager step forward. Morgan's arms came up, and she was inside them, releasing a deep-throated moan as her breasts crushed into him. She curled her arms around him, cupping her hands around his bottom, kneading his flesh. His jeans frustrated her. She didn't want denim. She wanted skin. She tucked her thumbs into his waistband, slid them around to the front and started working on his buckle.

Morgan grunted in surprise. His arms tightened around her, "Just a minute here, Lacy. If we're going to do this, we're going to do it right."

She got the belt undone, then attacked the snap of his jeans. "I don't think there's a wrong way to do it."

"I don't know about that. I don't have a clear understanding of what you mean by sexual incompatibility, but I'm not going to let either of us rush through this. We're going to take it slow and easy."

"Whatever." The snap opened. Her fingers closed around the metal of his zipper. Slow and easy could take a hike. Now that she was committed, she was eager for it to happen.

Morgan chuckled softly and grabbed her wrists. "How about if we start with taking off your clothes?" Without waiting for an answer, he released her hands and used his to untie the sash of her housecoat. It fell open, leaving her standing in front of him in her peach-colored pajamas. She should have worn something else, Lacy thought. Something black and slinky, maybe. Unfortunately, she didn't own anything black and slinky—and she wasn't about to make a trip into town now to pick something up.

Morgan didn't seem to mind. He studied her up and down, then slid an arm underneath her housecoat and pulled her to him. His mouth, when he kissed her, was hard and hot and eager, while his hand felt for the hem of her pajama top, then slipped underneath, over her naked back. Lacy shuddered at the feel of his hand on her. Then he removed his hand from her back and unfastened the top button on her pajamas. Lacy stood still, her heart thudding in eager anticipation as he popped open the next one, and then the next. By the time he'd undone them all, she was trembling.

Morgan slowly widened the gap he'd created, easing the material off her shoulders. Lacy was barely aware of it leaving her arms. Morgan's eyes were dark blue now. His cheeks were ruddy and he was breathing as heavily as she was. "You're real pretty, honey," he mumbled thickly. Lacy shivered, either because the room was cold or because of the expression on his face. He put his hands on her waist, then stroked upward, gently fingering her breasts before taking one in his palm. He groaned, pulled her closer and lowered his head to her ear. "I've been wanting to get you in a bedroom for some time."

"I'm here now," Lacy got out in a voice that was so guttural she hardly recognized it as her own.

Morgan backed her against the bed, then tumbled onto it, taking her with him. He landed on top of her, pinning her with his weight. His mouth closed over one of her breasts, sucking hard, and she squirmed under him, moaning. She was vaguely aware of him sliding her pajamas down around her knees. He propped himself up on an elbow and slid a palm along her length, over the soft curve of her stomach to the sensitive curls below, then used a thumb and forefinger to part her. He held her open and stroked a finger from his other hand into her. His thumb found the throbbing flesh above her opening. He touched it lightly, then, when she gasped with startled pleasure, stroked it again. Lacy groaned and arched up against him in a silent plea for more. Morgan lowered his head and kissed her. "Like I said, we're going to take it slow and easy."

"Morgan..."

His mouth covered hers again, his tongue sliding in and out of her mouth in the same rhythm his finger was using, stroking in and out of her body. Lacy lay helpless under him, her entire focus on the movement of his hands, the press of his body, the sensation of his tongue filling her mouth. She moved in an instinctive rhythm with him, her only thought how much she liked it and how much she never wanted him to stop.

He stopped and rolled away from her.

Lacy dragged up her thousand-pound eyelids to see him standing beside the bed, looking down at her while he stripped off his jeans. "I'd say you're hot enough, honey, and I sure am." He reached for a drawer beside his bed and pulled out a small square packet. "We're not starting any kids before we're married," he announced firmly. "I'm real clear on that."

Lacy hardly heard him. She was staring at the fully aroused, totally naked male body a few feet away from her. His thighs were as magnificent as she'd imagined...and so was the rest of him. He was a big man. It was only to be expected that he'd be big all over, but she'd never thought about that part of his anatomy. Now she couldn't think of anything else.

He yanked her pajamas the rest of the way off, tossed them on the floor, knelt between her thighs and filled his hands with her hips, pulling her up to him. His eyes glittered with passion and with another emotion—a primitive, masculine possessiveness that even in her passion-drugged state Lacy could recognize. A warning bell went off in the back of her lust-filled mind. This was not a good idea. Morgan was going to take this to mean a lot more than it did. Maybe she shouldn't have—

Then he thrust into her and she forgot what she was thinking. He was everywhere, inside her, around her, on top of her, his scent oozing into her nostrils, his breath harsh and demanding against her ear, and all she could think about was the movement of his body as he stroked in and out of her, the rasp of his thighs against hers, the sensations he was creating in her aroused body. The tension inside her grew as they moved together and apart, together and apart, until she couldn't stand it anymore. There was one instant of awareness that it was going to happen, and then she was clutching his shoulders, shuddering into climax, groaning out his name in a guttural voice that she'd never heard before. Morgan gathered her up and held her to him, surging in and out of her twice more before he was doing the same thing.

Lacy lay very still afterward. She'd just made love with Morgan Brillings and it had been spectacular.

After a few minutes, Morgan gave her cheek a kiss, rolled off her and rearranged the blanket so it was covering her before going into the bathroom. Lacy stayed where she was. She should, she supposed, go back to her own bedroom. She'd found out what she wanted to find out. There was no reason to spend the night with him. She couldn't summon the energy to move, though—and it seemed rude to scamper off, leaving him to return to an empty bed. She closed her eyes. She'd just lie there for a couple of minutes. Then she'd leave.

Morgan returned to the room, tossed back the covers and climbed in, lying flat on his back beside her. His arm came up to circle her shoulders. "Are you all right, honey?"

"Uh-huh."

"What do you think? Are you still wondering about this sexual compatibility thing?"

Lacy had pretty much forgotten about that. "No."

"You don't think it's going to be a problem?"

Lacy was glad of the darkness. She was positive she was blushing. "No."

"Good."

He fell silent. Lacy closed her eyes. She felt better than she had for ages. Then she recalled the expression she'd seen in Morgan's eyes. She should say something—or do something—to make sure he realized that this didn't mean she'd decided to marry him. She listened to his deep, even breathing. He must be asleep. Waking him up to impart this information didn't seem right. Besides, she wasn't quite sure how to put it.

Hovering on the edge of sleep, she tried to order her lazy muscles to get her out of there when Morgan spoke again. "Lacy?"

"Hmmm?"

"I'm not sure about this."

Lacy rolled on her side to peer through the darkness at him. "You're not sure about what?"

"This sexual compatibility thing." His eyes were closed, but the hand that roamed down her back and around the curve of her buttocks indicated that he wasn't asleep. "It could be that we should take a little more time to find out."

She should *not* do this, Lacy realized. She should say no and leave the room. He gave her bottom a gentle squeeze, jolting her body into excited anticipation. His leg moved, inserting itself between hers. There was still a lot of his body she hadn't explored, Lacy rationalized. And he did have a point. Just because it was great once didn't mean it would be great the second time.

She stroked a hand down his chest, then down farther, across his tummy and through a nest of fine, wiry hair, until her fingers found his erection. "You might be right."

11

THERE MUST BE HUNDREDS of ways for a woman to convince a man she wasn't going to marry him, Lacy ruminated the next morning.

Spending the night with him, engaged in a lot of hot and heavy sex, probably wasn't one of them.

She stood in the doorway of Morgan's dishwasherless kitchen, watched Morgan whistle through his teeth as he scrambled eggs. She'd woken to find herself alone in his bed, with the sun streaming through his window, indicating that it was well past her usual rising time. She'd had a quick shower and pulled on her clothes while trying to put the events of the preceding night into perspective. Yes, she'd slept with him. Yes, it had felt good. However, that's all there was to it.

She doubted Morgan realized this. He looked relaxed and smug this morning—too darn smug as a matter of fact. He turned, caught sight of her and grinned. "Good morning there, Lacy." His gaze, warm and possessive, wandered over her before he continued on with his task.

"Morning," Lacy mumbled. She felt a little uneasy around him—as if she wasn't quite sure how to act. That was because of her lack of experience in this sort of thing. She should have read up on it before she'd done it.

Morgan didn't appear to share her discomfort. "There was no reason for you to get up this early," he advised in a casual, conversational tone. "You could have stayed in bed if you had a mind to."

I would have if you'd been there. Lacy shoved the unworthy thought aside. After the night they'd spent together, she'd expected to be over her sexual fascination with him. Instead, she wanted more.

Of course, it was partly Morgan's fault. He looked darn good this morning, with his hair still damp from his shower, wearing a clean white-and-gray Western shirt and his customary snug-fitting jeans. Stirringly good. Compellingly good. Knowing how he looked under those clothes was compelling, as well.

She poured herself a cup of coffee and settled into a chair. "I should have been up hours ago. I've got a lot to do today."

"Oh?" Morgan set a plate of food in front of her, then took the seat opposite. "I figured you could spend the morning here. We've got a lot of details to settle."

Tempted by the idea of a whole day with him, Lacy hesitated. "I can't. I need to go to my own place. I've got my own cattle to keep an eye on and—"

"No need to worry about that," Morgan said easily. "Eddie is handling it."

"Eddie?"

"Uh-huh. I sent him over there first thing this morning to take care of the chores." He chuckled. "He couldn't wait to go, either. I think he was glad to get away from me for a little while. He's packing the cell phone, so you can give him a call and tell him what you want done. He's a good hand, but he's got the memory of a rabbit."

"Oh." Lacy searched for another excuse. "Well, uh, I'd like to go into town and check on my father."

Morgan nodded agreement. "He's doing fine. I called the hospital this morning to check on him."

"I'd still like to see him."

"So would I. We'll both go in to see him later."

Lacy squirmed. "I'd also like to drop in to see Janice. She was going to see if she could track down one of Sarah Larkspur's relatives."

"Sure," Morgan said. "I'll run you over there and pick you up on our way into town."

Lacy had another errand to run—one she was positive he wasn't going to like. She might as well get the fireworks over now. "And I planned on going back to the place where Dad got shot to take another look around."

Morgan's mug hit the table with a bang. "There's no way in hell," he said flatly.

Lacy's ire rose. She might have anticipated this reaction, but she didn't appreciate it. Morgan was way too sure of himself. He seemed to think that just because she spent one night with him, he could tell her what to do. If he was like this before they were married, what would he be like after? "There's no reason not to go. Dwight said his men were going to check out the area. If they found something, I'm sure they'd have called."

Morgan frowned. "There's no way two men can cover that area in less than a week—and even then you can't be sure they haven't missed something."

Lacy got to her feet, agitated. "Look, Morgan, I don't have a death wish here or anything. I don't want anyone to shoot at me again. But it seems pretty darn strange that all the action seems to be happening out where I saw that ghost."

Morgan looked troubled. "I agree with you on that point. But you're not going out there and that's final." He got up. "If you want that area checked out, I'll do it."

A vision of Morgan sitting on the ground with a bullet in his shoulder flashed across Lacy's mind. She shuddered. "There's no way in hell!" she retorted, unwittingly repeating his earlier response.

Morgan's jaw dropped. "What was that?"

"You heard me." She faced him down, eyes flashing as she advanced on him. "If it's not safe for me to go there, it's not safe for you to go, either!"

His jaw tightened and twin flags of brilliant red rose in his cheeks. "Now look here, Lacy—"

"I said no, Morgan, and I mean it. *N. O.*"

"Damn it, Lacy!"

Lacy folded her arms and stood her ground.

"Well, I'll be," he said, studying her through narrowed eyes. "Are you going to be this difficult after we're married?"

"I certainly am, and it's not settled that we're getting married."

"Damn it all to hell," he said. He sat back down and stared at her. "It looks like we're going to have to establish a few ground rules here."

Lacy nodded. "Yes, we are. And one of them is that if you get to tell me what I can do, I get to tell you what you can do."

Morgan opened his mouth to answer back, but his words were interrupted by a knock on the door. He growled an oath and stomped out of the room to answer it. Lacy watched him go, then dropped, breathless and triumphant, into a chair. She'd won that round. Now that Morgan realized what it was going to be like, he might not be so keen on marrying her.

For some reason, that didn't thrill her a whole lot.

There was the sound of voices from the other room, then Morgan's footsteps as he returned to the kitchen. When he reached the doorway, he had an odd expression on his face. "There's a...er...fellow here to see you."

"To see me?" Lacy got up. "Who is it?"

"I believe he said his name is Lieutenant Woodlow."

"Lieutenant?"

"Yup." Morgan rolled his eyes. "He stopped by your place and Eddie met him with a shotgun. I don't know what's the matter with that boy, Lacy. He should know he can't take on the whole U.S. Navy."

"I DON'T BELIEVE THIS," Lacy muttered. She stared out the window at the departing olive green military truck. "I saw a ghost, so you called the *navy?*"

Morgan looked as flummoxed as she felt. "I didn't call 'em, honey. That was Wade's doing. He sent them here."

"I know." The lieutenant had been real clear on that. He'd explained that Commander Brillings wanted them to carry out a set of standard maneuvers on Lacy's ranch—concentrating their efforts on the area where Lacy had seen the ghost. They were to keep on the lookout for any sign of rustlers—or anything else, no matter how small, out of the ordinary.

Apparently, Morgan's brother didn't realize that a bunch of navy strongmen searching her land was an oddity itself.

Neither did the lieutenant. He'd acted as if the whole thing made perfect sense. He wouldn't even be bothering Lacy about it except that he needed her to sign permission for them to do it. Lacy had signed. She couldn't think of any reason not to.

She plopped onto the sofa and swung her feet up to the coffee table. "I can't believe Wade did that."

"Neither can I." Morgan settled down beside her. His feet joined hers on the coffee table. "I suppose I should have, though. He's always been a mite peculiar. And he's getting more that way now that he's gotten married." He turned his head to look at her, his eyes widening at a thought. "You don't suppose that's going to happen to me, do you?"

Lacy didn't feel like having another "We're not getting married" discussion. "I wouldn't think so," she said instead.

"I hope not." Morgan shook his head. "I don't know what's come over him this time. According to the lieutenant, he's all bent out of shape, positive that some no-account rustler is going to take a shot or two at me." He looked both astonished and delighted at this display of brotherly affection. "He even sent me one of those bulletproof vests they use when they're out at sea. He told the lieutenant that if some idiot was around here taking shots at folks, he was going to make darn sure his only brother didn't catch a bullet."

"That's, uh, sweet," Lacy muttered, feeling a pang of regret that she was an only child.

"It is, isn't it?" Morgan gave her shoulder a possessive pat. "When we get around to having kids, let's make sure we have a couple of 'em. That way they can take care of each other."

"Morgan—"

"Plenty of time to talk about that later, honey." He jumped to his feet. "I'd best give Eddie a call and warn him that the navy is on their way back."

Lacy made a face as she watched him stride out of the room. She appreciated what Morgan and Wade were doing and really hoped that a search of the area would find something worthwhile. However, she was going to have to do something about the possessive gleam in Morgan's eye and his "Now everything is settled between us" attitude.

She didn't realize how serious the situation was, though, until they stopped by the hospital to check on Walt. He was still in bed when they got there, but there was color in his face, and his heart, the doctor told them, was ticking away just fine. However, they wanted to keep him there another night just to make sure.

Walt wasn't pleased about that—and he wasn't too thrilled when Lacy told him about the navy personnel searching their property, either. "I don't know what they think they're going to find there," he grumbled. "There's nothing on that land except rocks and bush. It's not even good cattle-grazing country."

Lacy patted his hand and gave her mother a sympathetic smile. "I don't think they're searching for grazing land, Dad. I think Wade sent them to flush out the rustlers."

"That's a waste of time. Any rustler with one lick of common sense would be long gone by now."

Rita looked up at the ceiling and shook her head. "I still think that's very sweet of Wade to do that for us, Walt."

Walt let out a bark of laughter. "I don't think it's got anything to do with us. It's more to do with Lacy."

"Me?" Lacy exclaimed, startled.

"Uh-huh." Her father's eyes twinkled at her, bright and knowing. "A man wants to take care of his own. Now that you're going to marry Morgan, Wade considers you family."

Lacy flushed at that and was suddenly glad that Morgan had tactfully left them alone for a few minutes. "I never said I was marrying Morgan, Dad. I said I'd think about it, that's all."

"Is that so?" Walt rubbed his jaw reflectively. "I understand you spent the night at his place."

Lacy ground her teeth. She'd known that was a mistake. "I stayed there because the sheriff—and Morgan—overreacted! It doesn't mean anything."

"That's not what I hear." Walt's grin was as smug as Morgan's had been. "Half the town has been in here to see me, and they've all been congratulating me on your engagement."

Lacy's stomach sank to her toes. "They have?"

"Yep."

Lacy gave her parents an accusing look. "How did anyone else find out?"

Rita rushed to reassure her. "We didn't tell them, Lacy. Honestly. They told us."

"Terrific." Lacy had no problem narrowing down who had spread the word—and he was waiting for her on the other side of the door. She got up. "Don't believe everything you hear," she warned her parents.

Her father looked alarmed. "Now, Lacy—"

"It's okay, Dad. I'll handle it." She kissed her parents goodbye and marched out of the room.

Morgan was sitting in a worn orange chair, his elbows on his knees, his hat in his hand. He got to his feet when he saw her. "Is everything all right?"

"Just fine," Lacy muttered. There were two nurses standing in the hall a few feet away, watching them with interest. They were local girls, well acquainted with both Morgan's family and her own. She'd wait until they were alone.

Morgan opened the truck door for her—a courtesy she'd now come to expect. That annoyed her, as well. This whole business was getting too darn familiar.

Morgan climbed in and slid the key into the ignition. Lacy put a hand on his wrist to stop him. "Just a minute, Morgan. I want to talk to you."

"Oh?"

"Yes. Just who have you told about this 'engagement' of ours?"

Morgan shrugged, casual and unconcerned. "I don't know. Wade, of course. I told you that."

"Uh-huh. And who else?"

"Well…" Morgan thought about it. "Eddie. I imagine he told Susan. Monica and Amy in there. And I might have mentioned it to Cal in passing."

"Terrific," Lacy muttered.

Morgan knitted his brow. "What's the problem, honey? Folks are going to know about it sooner or later."

"They aren't if there's nothing to know about. And there isn't. Nothing is settled between us."

"What are you talking about? Of course things are settled. Last night—"

"Last night we slept together. You must have slept with other women—and you didn't marry them."

Morgan scowled. "No, I didn't. But none of them was you."

"That doesn't make any difference."

"It does to me! And it does to you, too. You don't normally go around spending the night with men, do you?"

Lacy flushed. "No, I don't. But I have done it and I didn't marry them."

"What exactly are you trying to tell me here? That last night was a one-night stand or something?"

"That's exactly what I'm trying to tell you. Just because we had sex doesn't mean I'm going to marry you. And I'll tell you something else. We are not, repeat not, going to do it again."

"Shit," Morgan said. He swung the truck to the right, then came to a jarring halt in front of the local pub.

"What are you doing?"

"We're stopping for a drink." Morgan yanked open his door. "Right about now, I could do with one."

A ONE-NIGHT STAND and they weren't going to do it again?

Morgan took a swig from the glass of beer in front of him and glowered at the woman sitting on the other side of the table. Lacy looked terrific tonight.

Her hair was loose around her shoulders instead of tied back, and she even had on a touch of makeup. He'd thought that was for his benefit. Apparently, he'd been wrong.

He had no idea why Lacy was acting this way. After the night they'd spent together, and the equally pleasant day, he'd figured things were settled between them. Instead, she'd made it clear that they weren't. Were all women this difficult, or was it just her?

His annoyance increased when Lacy turned the conversation around to one of her favorite subjects—Jake Malone.

"You won't believe what Janice found out about him," she enthused. Morgan could think of several other topics he'd rather discuss, like why she'd slept with him if she didn't plan on marrying him, but there was no stopping Lacy once she got started. "She managed to track down one of Sarah Larkspur's descendants."

"Oh, yeah?"

"Uh-huh." Lacy's eyes glittered with excitement. "He had a couple of letters Sarah wrote to his grandmother. He faxed them to Janice. It's really interesting, Morgan."

Morgan wasn't interested in anything other than getting her back in his bed so he could settle this marriage business once and for all. "How's that?"

Lacy settled back. "Well, in these letters, Sarah mentions the problems she's had with Karl, and how this man—Jake Malone—showed up one day to help her."

"Did she say why she thought Karl was giving her so much grief?"

Lacy nodded. "She did. It was because of the silver mine on her property."

Morgan shook his head. "There's no silver mine anywhere around here."

"Yes, there is. There's that one on Cal's place. Janice and I think that's the one Sarah was referring to."

Morgan considered that. It made sense. Cal had told Lacy that he now owned all the former Larkspur land. "That mine was played out years ago."

"It probably wasn't when Sarah was alive," Lacy countered. "In any case, that's the reason Karl wanted Sarah's land. After Jake shot Karl, Sarah had the mine boarded up. Apparently, she wasn't interested in mining. She was just interested in ranching."

"So what happened to Jake?" Morgan asked, more to keep the conversation going than because he cared.

"I don't know." Her eyes got that dreamy, faraway look that was becoming all too familiar. "He rode off into the sunset, I suppose."

That didn't sound like something to make her look so goosey. "And?" Morgan prompted.

"And...nothing. He just rode off, that's all." She sighed again. "Isn't it romantic? A handsome, mysterious stranger shows up and helps the rancher's daughter save her ranch. Then he rides off into the sunset never to be seen again."

Morgan still didn't get it. "What in hell is so romantic about that? He left her all alone! If he had given a damn about Sarah, he wouldn't have left her to run the place all by herself!"

"That was probably what she wanted."

"Is that so? Well, in that case, I'd say she wasn't too bright."

Lacy rolled her eyes. "You just don't understand."

He sure didn't. None of this made one lick of sense to him. He watched Lacy's eyes cloud over as she gazed off into the distance and he gritted his teeth. There she went again, getting all goosey about a man she'd never met. Lord, he was tired of that. He was right here, damn it, but did she get that look in her eye about him? Nope. Even after the night they'd spent together, a night of darn good sex, she didn't get that look about him. As a matter of fact, she'd told him flat out that it was just a one-night stand. A one-night stand, for chrissake! His jaw tightened. He was getting mighty close to being annoyed with her.

He stood abruptly and grabbed her wrist. "Let's dance."

Lacy didn't move. He ignored her surprised exclamation and propelled her out onto the dance floor. He wasn't a great dancer, but he could sure as hell outdance a ghost!

He pulled her against him and felt a small, delicious tremor go through her before she could hide it. That made him feel better. Apparently, dancing wasn't the only thing he could do better than a ghost. He wouldn't mind taking her on home and giving her a demonstration, but that wasn't going to happen. She'd made it clear that last night had only been a one-night stand to her. Then again, maybe she needed a little reminding about how much she'd enjoyed that "one-night stand."

He lowered his head until his lips were right beside her ear. "That was just a one-night stand, huh?"

Lacy shivered again, but her voice was cool when she spoke. "That's right."

"That's a darn shame." He swung her around, then pulled her up against him again and nuzzled his head down against her ear so only she could hear him. "I was looking forward to making love to you again tonight."

She flushed. "Morgan—"

"I was going to start by taking off your shirt." He slid a hand between them and closed his palm around her breast, then moved it away when she stiffened. "I'd take it off real slow, button by button. Then I'd start working on your bra." He touched her bra clasp briefly. "I'd pull it down a little so it was just below your breasts. Then I'd start touching them. You like it when I touch them, don't you?"

Lacy's head swirled as she took a frantic look around. "Morgan, you can't talk like that. People will—"

"Then I'd use my tongue on them." He gritted his teeth as he thought about her bare breasts, her nipples straining against his mouth. "I like the way you taste, Lacy. I like feeling your breast in my mouth."

She took a sharp intake of air.

Morgan kept right on talking. "All the time I was doing that, I'd be holding you against me." He lowered his hand to her buttocks and pushed her against him, letting her feel how aroused he was getting. "I'd start taking off your jeans...real slow, like I did your shirt. I'd get 'em down, oh, maybe to your knees, and then I'd start working on your panties."

"Stop this right now, Morgan!"

"Soon as I got a finger or two up inside you, I'd start stroking. In and out." He pressed her against him, then released her in time with his words. "In and out. In and out. And all the while I was doing that, I'd be sucking on your breasts."

She was breathing heavy now, panting against him, clinging to him.

"I'd do that until you couldn't stand it anymore. Then maybe I'd let you touch me. Feel how much I want you." The notion of her palms around him made his breath catch. "I'd sure enjoy that, Lacy. I'd enjoy that a whole lot."

She sagged against him.

"We'd be so hot, honey, that I wouldn't be able to wait much longer. I'd want to be inside you, feeling you close around me, listening to you make those little noises in your throat that get me so hard it hurts." He gave her a little squeeze. "You listening to me, Lacy?"

"Yes," she breathed.

"Good. Because then I'd be moving, trying to get as far inside you as I could get, pushing in and pulling out, in and out, in and out." He put his lips right beside her ear. "You with me here?"

"I, uh, uh…"

"That's how it would happen." The music stopped. He released her. There! Let her spend the night thinking about that! "But it's not going to happen because last night was just a one-night stand!"

Before she could answer, he put an arm around her waist and half carried her back to their table. Lacy dropped into her chair and took a deep breath, clearly struggling for control. Morgan was still annoyed with her. Trying to recover, was she? Well, he wasn't going let that happen.

"You about ready to go?" he asked.

She shook her head. "No, I—"

"We really should be on our way." Morgan picked up his hat. "I've got to get you home, then drive on over to my place."

He took her hand and marched out the door with her in tow. She was totally silent although he could hear her breathing heavily. Good. He hoped she suffered all goddamn night.

He wrenched open the truck door. "Hop in."

Lacy looked up at him, her eyes wide and luminous in the moonlight. "Listen, Morgan, I, uh, might have been a bit hasty back there."

Morgan raised an eyebrow. "How's that?"

"I just, uh, I mean..." She licked her lips and eyed him from head to toe. "About that one-night-stand thing..."

Morgan shoved a thumb in his belt in an attempt to ease his straining jeans. "Oh?"

"No." Her tongue came out to touch her lips. "Maybe we could consider it the first night of...of an affair."

Morgan wasn't quite ready to forgive her. "You reckon so?"

Lacy nodded.

He nodded once and opened his arms. Lacy launched herself against him in a mass of flying hair, wrapping her arms around him, thrusting her pelvis against his. Morgan kissed her hard while she squirmed against his body. "All right, then," he said gruffly. He gripped her tightly and kissed her with determined passion until her mouth trembled under his and she sagged against him. "Let's go home, honey."

Morgan hadn't driven this fast since he was a teenager. He made the twenty-minute drive in less than fifteen. "Just hurry," Lacy urged.

There was no way in hell he was going to hurry. He was going to have her weak and quivering in his arms all night. Maybe that would get her mind off her ghostly gunslinger.

Lacy was out of the truck as soon as he stopped in front of his house. Morgan jumped out, rounded the truck and grabbed her wrist. "Hang on there, Lacy."

She looked up at him, her eyes dark with lust. "But we need to…we—"

"Seems to me we've got a little unfinished business." He pushed her back against the truck and held her there with his hips. Then he started working on the buttons of her blouse. "Remember how I said I was going to do this?"

"Yes, but…but we're outside."

"I never said I was going to do it inside, did I?"

She glanced around wildly. "But we can't…we can't…someone might see us and—"

"There isn't anyone here to see us. Eddie and Susan are five miles away. There's no one around here but a few critters."

"I still don't think…" He got the next button undone and grazed his thumb across a nipple. Lacy moaned.

"You don't think what?" Morgan prompted as he undid another button.

"It's not a-a-appropriate."

Morgan slid his hands inside the slash of her blouse and felt his way to the back of her bra. "I think it is." He unfastened the bra, tugged it downward, baring both breasts, then closed the thumb and forefinger of each hand around her nipples. They were already hard and distended. He rolled them between his fingers, watching her expression all the while.

Lacy closed her eyes and sucked in a breath through her parted lips. He lowered his head to take a breast in his mouth. Gasping she arched her back. "Maybe you're right."

After that, it was just how he described. He used his mouth and his tongue on her breasts until she was whimpering and squirming. Then he unfastened her jeans, pulled down her panties and used his fingers. She shuddered and moaned and braced herself back against his truck, thrusting her hips forward.

That gave Morgan another idea. He scooped her up and slid her across the warm hood of the truck. He pulled off her boots one by one, then tugged her jeans down her legs. When he had dropped them on the ground, he grasped her panties in both hands and slowly rolled them down her legs, then stepped into the V of her thighs. She stared up at him, her eyes gleaming in the darkness. "What?"

"I'll show you." He used his tongue on her, holding her hips firmly in place. Her taste drove him wild, her cries of pleasure went straight to his head and then to his groin, but it was the stiffening of her body, followed by shudders as she climaxed, that pleased him the most.

He released her and looked down at her face. It was soft in the moonlight, her eyes dazed and satisfied. "Wow," she said. "That was amazing. I don't think I've ever felt like that before."

Morgan slid an arm under her knees, another under her back, and picked her up. "Get used to it," he rumbled. "You're going to be feeling like that all night—over and over again."

He carried her into the bedroom, dropped her on the bed and started taking off his clothes. Lacy just lay there, watching him. Then, to his surprise, she bounded up and threw herself into his arms, tumbling him down on the bed with her. "If I'm going to feel like that, you're going to feel like that," she told him. She gave his briefs a downward tug, closed one palm around him and then, unexpectedly, took him in her mouth.

Morgan groaned with pleasure and collapsed back down. That was the problem with women, he decided. Everything you did to them backfired.

Lacy raised her head to look at him. "What?"

"Never mind, honey." He stretched out comfortably. "You just go on doing what you're doing. Most of the surprises aren't too hard to take."

"Remember," Lacy warned, "this is just about…about affairs."

Morgan wasn't going to let that bother him. He was positive he could turn this into a real engagement by the end of the week.

12

If SPENDING THE NIGHT with a man wasn't a good way to convince him she wasn't going to marry him, Lacy shouldn't have expected spending two nights with him to work.

Which was a good thing, because it hadn't.

She sat in Morgan's office late the next morning, with her chair pulled up beside his, examining at an aerial map showing both her property and his. "We can use this area to grow feed," Morgan suggested. He jabbed at the map with one long, tanned finger. "That would free up this area over here on your place to graze cattle."

"That's too big an area, Morgan. If we did that, we'd have to start raising horses because we'd be riding all day and all night."

"All day, maybe," Morgan drawled. "I've got other plans for the nights."

Lacy felt the blood rise in her cheeks. "We shouldn't make too many plans," she warned. "We haven't decided for sure that we're going to get married."

"Uh-huh," Morgan said, looking not the least bit perturbed.

"We're still…thinking about it."

"Uh-huh." He tossed his pen onto the desktop

and stood. "I need some more coffee. How about you?"

Lacy sighed and gave up. No matter what she said, Morgan still believed that everything was settled between them. "I'm fine," she muttered. She watched him leave the room, then added, "Stupid but fine."

"Stupid" was the operative word. This thing with Morgan was getting out of hand. It was her own fault, of course. She shouldn't have spent last night with him, and she really shouldn't be spending this time with him, discussing property amalgamation, either.

She hadn't intended to do this. Before she'd fallen asleep last night, she'd firmly resolved to pack her things and return to her place today. There was no logical reason for her not to do that. Wade had half the navy scouring the area. With that many armed men around, she didn't think anyone was going to take a shot at her or anybody else.

But that hadn't happened. Morgan had been beside her when she woke up and had immediately swept her off into another bout of passionate lovemaking. That had been followed by an easy, comfortable breakfast, during which he'd captured her interest by claiming an unusual problem with one of his calves. Since Eddie was still at her place, there were a number of chores to do here. After they'd finished those, he'd lured her into this amalgamation discussion.

The really scary part was that Lacy was enjoying it. She was also having weird thoughts about how they could rearrange the furniture and where she could put that cute little table her grandmother had left her. At lunchtime, she'd even found herself thinking about making a batch of cookies.

It wasn't a total transformation, she reassured herself. When she went back to her own place, she'd revert to her normal, sensible self. There'd be lots of hard work to do, which would help her to overcome her obsession with Morgan.

And with any luck at all, the navy would find something fabulously wonderful—the same something Jake had been trying to show her—that would save her ranch so she didn't have to get married.

That's what she needed now—for Wade's version of the cavalry and her ghostly gunslinger to rescue her.

IT WAS AFTER TWO when the navy boys showed up at Morgan's doorstep to report on their findings.

Lacy was in the barn at the time, working on repairing one of the stalls. Morgan called her inside, and they both listened in silence as the lieutenant informed them that, after an exhaustive search of the area, they had turned up...absolutely nothing.

Not quite nothing. "We did find a few shell casings," he admitted. "And there were signs that someone has been in the area recently. They could have been cattle rustlers, I suppose—but if so, they've cleared out by now."

Morgan released a breath he didn't realize he'd been holding. "You're sure about that?"

"Yes, sir. My men are thorough." His lips twitched slightly. "Besides, if we're wrong, we'd have Commander Brillings breathing down our necks. That gives us a lot of motivation."

Morgan winced, a tad embarrassed by Wade's display of concern.

"Not that I blame him," the lieutenant added. "I've got a brother myself. I wouldn't want to see anything happen to him."

"Appreciate it," Morgan said. He glanced over at Lacy. She was sitting very still, staring at the navy boy's report, while the color slowly seeped out of her face. Her reaction puzzled him, but before he could ask her about it, the lieutenant was speaking again.

"We'll clear off your land now, ma'am."

"All right," Lacy mumbled. She looked up. "Thank you."

"You're welcome." He turned to leave, then stopped. "By the way, you might want to consider boarding up that old mine that's down there. It looks as if someone's been in it and a few of the boards are broken. You don't want anyone to get hurt."

"Mine?" Morgan shook his head. "There's no mine on Lacy's property."

"There's a mine there," the lieutenant insisted. "It's plenty old, but it's there."

Morgan opened his mouth to argue, then closed it again. The lieutenant reminded him of a young Wade and there'd never been any point in arguing with Wade.

Still wondering about it, he accompanied the lieutenant to the door, shook the man's hand and watched him leave. When he returned to the living room, Lacy was still sitting on the sofa, rereading the report.

Morgan stopped in front of her. "What mine do you suppose that fellow was talking about?"

Lacy shook her head. "I don't know. They must have strayed onto Cal's property. Remember that old silver mine he's got out there?"

"I suppose." That was a logical explanation, although Morgan found it hard to believe. There's no way Wade would make a mistake like that. He wouldn't have thought Wade's men would do it, either. He shoved the puzzle aside as unimportant and concentrated on the woman in front of him. "Are you all right?"

"I'm fine." She sighed and collapsed back against the cushions. "I just can't believe they didn't find anything. I was so sure."

Morgan sat down beside her. "What did you expect them to find?"

"I don't know. Something."

She looked tremendously disappointed, a reaction Morgan didn't understand. He took her hand. It was icy cold, as if she'd just received a great shock. "This is good news, Lacy. There aren't any rustlers out there, and the men found nothing else, either. We can stop worrying that someone shot at you and Walt on purpose."

"I guess." She stared at her hand in his, then extracted it and jumped to her feet. "Can I borrow one of your trucks? I'd like to drop in on Janice. I promised her I'd let her know what the navy found out."

"Go ahead." He fished the keys out of his pocket and tossed them to her. "Just bring it back in one piece."

She managed a faint smile. "I will." She started out of the room, then stopped at the doorway and turned around. "Oh, and when my parents come home, I guess we should start discussing wedding plans."

She was out the door before Morgan could say anything.

He stood at the window, watching her drive away, then sat back down on the sofa. *I guess we should start discussing wedding plans,* she'd said. That had to mean she'd finally realized they weren't just having an affair. This was a permanent thing. He felt a sudden burst of elation that almost immediately faded. She hadn't looked like someone who wanted to get married. She'd looked like—well, like she'd seen a ghost.

He picked up the report the navy officer had left and absently thumbed through it while he reviewed Lacy's behavior. She'd been clearly disappointed that they hadn't found anything. She'd been hoping they would. As he turned it over in his mind, Morgan suddenly realized what she'd been thinking. She'd figured that if the navy found something worth having on her land, then she wouldn't have to marry him. It wasn't something she wanted to do. She was just going to do it so she could save her ranch—and those goddamn cattle of hers. That's all she'd ever really cared about—that and her gun-slinger.

His efforts to make her fall in love with him hadn't worked. She wasn't in love with him. She wasn't going to be looking at him with stars in her eyes the way Cassie looked at Wade. He wasn't even sure Lacy was capable of doing that. She didn't want to get married—not to him or to anyone. Lacy wanted what Sarah Larkspur had had—a gunslinger who would save her ranch, then disappear into the sunset.

Too bad Malone wasn't around now to do it for her.

He took another look at the report. There wasn't one thing in there that would suggest anything valuable was on Lacy's land. He paused at the part about the mine. Too bad that mine wasn't filled with silver—and sitting on Lacy's property.

Of course, who said it wasn't?

He stretched back and closed his eyes. He was probably getting as squirrelly as Wade and Lacy. Still, the possibility of another mine did exist. It probably wasn't worth anything, but it wouldn't hurt to check into it.

He went into his office, picked up the phone and dialed Cal's number. "That old mine of yours," he said after they'd exchanged pleasantries. "Have you been doing some work on it?"

Cal chuckled. "Good Lord, no. There's nothing in there. Hasn't been for years. Why?"

Morgan took a breath. "Well, you know how the navy's been taking a look around Lacy's place?"

"I heard about that, yes. I don't know what they thought they'd find. Any self-respecting rustler would be long gone by now."

"They are," Morgan assured him. "But they did stumble across a mine out there. They mentioned it needed to be boarded up. Now, I know darn well there isn't one on Lacy's land. I figured they must have been talking about yours."

Cal's voice came back quick—a shade to quick as a matter of fact. "Yes. Yes, they must have been. I'll fix it up right away."

It could have been the heartiness in Cal's voice or maybe just his too quick response. Whatever it was, something about it made Morgan uneasy as he hung up the phone. It was a pretty far-fetched theory, but if there was another mine out there, and Cal's great-great-uncle had known about it, then there was a pretty good chance that Cal knew about it, too.

Which might give him a darn good motive for wanting the Johnsons off their land.

Morgan got to his feet and started out the door. He might not be Lacy's gunslinger, but he might be able to help her out yet.

JANICE WAS ALMOST as disappointed as Lacy. "I can't believe they didn't find anything," she exclaimed. "Even Oliver thought they would."

"Did he?" Lacy noticed that Janice's eyes went soft when she said Oliver's name.

"What are you going to do now?"

Lacy shrugged. "I guess I'll get married." She made a face, although the idea wasn't as repellent as it had been when Morgan first suggested it. It wouldn't be all that bad. There would be lots of nights like last night—and she'd enjoyed that. Morgan was a passable cook—and he was a naturally tidy man. They could get a new fridge. She could spruce up his place a little...even sleep in every now and then.

And say goodbye to all her plans for running her ranch herself. That would not happen. Morgan was like every other man around here—a standard, run-of-the-mill, take-charge cowboy who'd want everything done his way. True, he listened to her suggestions, but in the end, he would be the one who made the decisions. Besides, if she was going to be brutally honest about it, she was scared. She was scared that if she wasn't careful, she'd turn into Janice. And she was terrified that she might even like it.

She rose to her feet. "I'd better get going. Mom and Dad are coming home tomorrow. I'll discuss wedding plans with them. Then you and I can go dress shopping."

Janice's eyes filled with concern. "Lacy, are you sure?"

"No, I'm not." Lacy shoved her hat onto her head. "But I can't think of any other way to keep my ranch." She gave her friend a hug. "Don't worry. Things will work out."

"I thought they already had," Janice said mournfully. "I was so sure Jake was trying to tell you something. And Oliver agreed with me."

"I guess Oliver can be wrong sometimes, too," Lacy muttered. She wandered out to Morgan's truck, climbed in and carefully headed down the road. If Jake hadn't been here to tell her about a hidden treasure, why had he been here? Had she just imagined the whole thing after all?

She stopped at an intersection, then steered the truck in the direction of her own ranch. No, she hadn't imagined Jake's ghost and she was positive he'd been trying to tell her something. Even Oliver thought so.

No matter how illogical it was, she wanted to take one more look out there herself.

The sun was close to setting by the time Morgan found the mine.

It wasn't easy to find. It was half-hidden by a rock outcropping, its boarded-up entrance covered with branches as if someone hadn't wanted it to be found. Morgan had to marvel again at how thorough the navy was. If they were this good on land, they'd be hell on wheels at sea.

They were right about the condition of it, too. The boards seemed to have been pulled away quite recently. As a matter of fact, it looked as if someone besides the navy had been here—at least within the past couple of days anyway.

Morgan set down his rifle and squatted to check the tracks. It wasn't just within the past couple of days. It was within the past couple of hours—or maybe even the past couple of minutes.

He got to his feet and turned around.

Cal Robinson was standing a few feet away, a bulky shape outlined by the fading sunlight. "I'm real sorry you found this place, Morgan. Real sorry."

He was holding a gun, Morgan realized. He looked from it up to Cal's face. "I'm not too pleased about it myself." He squinted at the burly rancher. "How long have you known about this, Cal?"

"I figured it out a few years ago," Cal admitted. "I stumbled across a few things that used to belong to Karl. It wasn't much, but enough to let me know there was a mother lode of silver somewhere out here." He gestured around with his gun. "I've been trying to find it for a while. And a couple of years ago, I struck pay dirt." His eyes gleamed across the growing darkness. "I took a few ore samples in to make sure. And it looks like this mine has enough silver to make me a wealthy man. A very wealthy man."

"It'll make someone wealthy. But it won't be

you." Morgan nodded toward the mine. "This property belongs to the Johnsons."

"It's going to belong to me." Cal spoke with complete confidence. "Once you're out of the way, the Johnson's won't have any choice but to sell out."

"And you'll be right there to buy up the place," Morgan charged.

"It's the only neighborly thing to do." He grimaced and shook his head. "I knew it was going to come to this as soon as you told me that you were fixing to marry Lacy. I've been trying to think of another way around it, but there isn't."

Morgan eyed his rifle, sitting just a few feet away. "Listen, Cal—"

Cal cocked his gun. "Don't make it any harder than it already is."

"I sure as hell don't plan on making it easy," Morgan snarled. He tensed his muscles, hoped for the best and dove for cover.

MORGAN'S BLACK quarter horse was tied to a fence post when Lacy arrived. Lacy studied it as she secured Intrigue. "What's Morgan doing out here?" she asked it. "I thought he'd be busy working on how best to amalgamate our properties."

The horse swished its tail, gave her a wild-eyed look, then stared toward the trees. A million goose bumps rose on Lacy's body.

"What on earth?" she whispered. She didn't know what was going on, but she had a really bad feeling about it.

She raced into the trees as visions of her father, lying on the ground with a bullet in his arm, came back to her. As she approached the outcropping of rocks, she could hear the faint sound of voices in the distance. Men's voices. Morgan's voice. She couldn't make out the words, but something in his tone told her that things were definitely not okay.

She flew toward the sound, pushing her way through the trees, scratching her face on the branches. She rounded a huge pine, then froze.

The scene that met her could have come from a movie. Morgan was standing beside a rock. Directly in front of him was Cal Robinson. He had a gun in his hand—a gun he was aiming right at Morgan. Lacy screamed something—she wasn't sure what. Morgan lunged sideways. Cal fired his gun, and Morgan crumpled to the ground.

Lacy opened her mouth and screamed again—a strangled sound of shock, outrage and disbelief. As Cal whipped around, she launched herself down the hill at him, shouting at the top of her lungs. "What are you doing? What…?" She reached him before he could fire again and began pummeling him with her fists. *"No! No! No!"*

Cal pushed her to the ground. "What in hell?"

"You shot him!" Lacy screeched, hardly able to believe it. "You shot him. You shot Morgan!"

"Uh-huh." Cal barely gave the body on the ground a second glance. "It's your fault, Lacy. If you'd sold the place to me, none of this would be necessary."

Lacy had no idea what was going on but now didn't strike her as a good time to figure it out. She scraped up a handful of dirt and flung it into Cal's face, catching him totally off guard. Cursing, he swiped at his eyes. Lacy rolled away. Then she was on her feet, racing through the brush and trees toward her horse. Cal never did have good taste in horseflesh. Intrigue could outrun his any day. All she had to do was reach him.

At first it looked like she might. She could hear Cal pounding after her, but she'd had a head start. She reached the clearing and threw herself across it, struggling to untie the reins, to gather them up, then the click of a gun cocking brought her up short. She glanced frantically over her shoulder. Cal was standing just inside the clearing. "I'm sorry, Lacy," he said. "Real sorry."

He started to squeeze the trigger. Lacy remained rooted to the ground.

A gunshot rang out—but it wasn't Cal who fired. His weapon flew to the ground, leaving him cradling his right hand in his left. He grunted in surprise and whirled in the direction of the shot. Lacy's eyes flew in that direction, as well, and she gasped.

There was another man in the clearing. The setting sun silhouetted his body but masked his features. He was six feet tall, dressed in jeans, a sou'wester, and a cowboy hat was jammed on his head. He was dusty and dirty, and he was carrying a long-barreled rifle, a rifle aimed directly at Cal. "Jake," she whispered.

Cal released an inarticulate sound of rage and lunged for his weapon.

Her rescuer cocked the rifle one-handed and fired it into the ground right beside the handgun. Then he cocked it again and fixed it on Cal's middle. There wasn't a single doubt in Lacy's mind that he would shoot Cal if he had to.

Cal must have realized that, as well. He stood

very still, staring at the apparition. The man waved his rifle toward the trees. "Get!" he snarled.

Cal turned and stumbled into the trees. Lacy ignored him, her attention on the cowboy now striding toward her. Her heart leaped in her chest. This was her hero—her handsome, mysterious stranger, the man of her dreams.

The sun slid down another notch, enough to make his features visible. It wasn't Jake Malone after all. It was Morgan.

DWIGHT WAS AS ASTONISHED at the whole business as Lacy had been. He sat in one of the chairs at Morgan's kitchen table, making notes and staring at them with wide, round eyes. "Cal was the one behind all those things that happened to the Johnsons. Cal?"

"It looks that way," Lacy said. She leaned against the back of her chair, still feeling a little lightheaded, although it had been a good two hours since Morgan had stepped out of the trees to save her. Frowning, she looked over at Morgan. He was sitting upright in his chair, looking mighty uncomfortable. "Are you sure you're all right?" she asked.

"I'm fine." Morgan shifted positions, wincing. "Although I've got to tell you, even with one of those bulletproof vests on, getting shot is no hell. I have no idea why Wade keeps doing it. I'm still finding it hard to breathe."

"Watching someone get shot isn't much fun, either," Lacy put in. She was going to have nightmares about that scene for a long, long time.

Dwight was still looking puzzled. "Why would Cal want to force you folks off your land?"

Lacy took a swallow from the glass of whiskey in her hand, shuddering as it burned its way down her throat. Morgan had poured them both a drink when they'd arrived here, assuring her that it would make her feel a whole lot better. Lacy hadn't expected it to work. There wasn't enough liquor in North America to make her feel better about this. One of their neighbors—someone she'd always considered a friend—had been trying to force them off their land. Not only that, but he'd also shot her father! It was a lot to take in. "Not a clue," she lied.

Dwight swiveled his head toward Morgan. "How about you?"

Morgan caught her eye. Lacy gave her head a slight shake and he shrugged. "I don't know, Dwight. You'd have to ask Cal."

"Cal's not saying anything that makes sense," Dwight grumbled. "My men picked him up an hour ago—not long after you called. He keeps going on and on about how some ghost shot him." He gave Lacy a quizzical look. "He did mention something about a silver mine that one of his relations knew about. He seems to be under the impression that it's on your property."

"He does?" Lacy watched the whiskey swirl around in her glass. "I don't know where he got that idea."

"It might be worth checking out," Dwight encouraged.

"It might be." Lacy hadn't spent much time thinking about it, but she knew darn well that she didn't want word to get out about that mine until she'd had a chance to discuss it with her parents. "I'd, uh, appreciate it if this didn't get out, Dwight. I wouldn't want someone else to get the same idea."

Dwight chuckled. "You don't have to worry about that. We're sure not going to spread it around. And as for Cal, well, I'd say he's got a long stretch in front of him with a few dozen psychiatrists. The man's gone right off the deep end." He snapped his notebook shut and stood. "I think that's all for tonight. I'll call you tomorrow if I have any more questions." He picked up his hat from the table and turned to Lacy. "Are you about ready to go?"

"Go?" Lacy repeated blankly.

Dwight nodded. "Morgan asked me if I could give you a lift home."

"He did?" She glanced over at Morgan, who nodded confirmation. "Oh." She hadn't planned the rest of the night, but she assumed she'd be spending it here. "Well, uh, sure. Okay. I'll be right with you. I'd just like to have a word with Morgan first."

"No problem," Dwight said easily. "I'll wait for you out in the car."

Lacy watched him leave the room, then turned to Morgan. "I don't have to go home right now," she said. "I mean, if you want me to stay, I can."

Morgan shook his head. "There's no reason why you can't stay at your place now. Cal won't be trying to hurt you anymore."

"I know, but you're hurt."

"I'll be fine."

It was almost as if he was trying to get rid of her. "I still think I should stay here and take care of you."

"There's no need for that." Morgan pushed back his chair and eased himself upright, wincing as he did so. "Besides, you shouldn't be staying overnight at my place anymore. It isn't right."

Lacy gave a little laugh. "What do you mean it isn't right? You didn't have any problem with it last night."

"Last night we were thinking about getting married. Now we aren't."

"We aren't?"

"No, we aren't." He looked her straight in the eye. "There's no reason for us to get married now."

"What?"

"There isn't. The only reason Cal would act so crazy to have that silver mine is because there's something worth having in it. You're going to be a wealthy woman, Lacy. You don't need to marry me to keep your ranch."

Lacy hadn't considered the implications of the silver mine. "I suppose not."

Morgan smiled crookedly. "You don't want to marry me, honey. You've been real clear on that. And as it turns out, I don't want to marry you, either."

Lacy couldn't believe her ears. "You don't?"

"Nope." Morgan held up a hand. "Now I'm not saying I don't have feelings for you. I do. As a matter of fact, I think I've probably been in love with you for some time. I just didn't know it. But you don't feel the same way about me, do you?"

"I...uh..."

"You don't," Morgan said flatly. "And I don't want a wife who doesn't feel that way about me. I want one who looks at me with stars in her eyes— the way Cassie looks at Wade. That isn't going to be you, is it, honey?"

Lacy couldn't think of a thing to say.

"That's what I thought," Morgan muttered. He handed over her brown hat. "You better get going. Dwight's waiting for you."

Numbly, Lacy followed him to the door. When they reached it, she looked up into his face. His features were tightly controlled, and his eyes looked dark and empty. "Good night, Morgan," she said. "Thanks for everything."

"You're welcome. You take care now."

"I will." She swallowed and tottered down the steps toward Dwight's car. When she reached it, she took one last look at him over her shoulder. Morgan was standing in the doorway. The light from behind silhouetted his long, lean body, and he looked more like her gunslinger than ever.

13

"THE RANCH IS SAVED and I don't have to get married," Lacy told Oscar. "Isn't that wonderful?"

Oscar stretched out in front of the fireplace and closed his eyes. Apparently, he didn't think it was all that wonderful. Lacy had brought him in here to keep her company. The place was too dark and too quiet with no one else around.

But that was all going to change tomorrow. Her father was getting out of the hospital, and he and her mother would be back at home. "I'll tell them all about the silver mine then," she informed Oscar. "We can start making plans. With a silver mine as collateral, I'll have no problem getting a bank loan." She could pay off all their bills, too. Her parents could buy a place in town. She could hire someone to live on the property.

Of course, there'd be a lot of other things to do, like contacting a mining company. Lacy made a face at that. She didn't relish the idea of mining activity on their land.

She gave Oscar a brisk pat and got to her feet. "It won't be that bad, Oscar. I'm sure there are new ways of mining that are ecologically sound. Besides, it's not as if we use that land out there for anything. And I'll get to keep the ranch. There'll be enough money to set up a trailer and hire someone to help me. I won't be here alone, so no one will have to worry about me."

She wandered into the kitchen and put the kettle on for tea. "Mom and Dad can buy a house in town and get all new furniture for it. They'll even have enough money to take a few trips, if that's what they want to do."

She'd be alone in this house, though. She'd spend her nights alone and she'd spend most of her days alone, as well. There would be no amalgamating properties or buying a new fridge or making wedding plans. None of that was going to happen.

She rinsed the teapot with boiling water and dropped in a tea bag. She didn't want that to happen. She didn't want to turn into Janice. On the other hand, Janice seemed pretty darn happy.

Making an exclamation of disgust, Lacy poured herself a cup of tea and carried it into the living room. Oscar was still stretched out in front of the fireplace. "I'm going to be perfectly happy here," she told him as she curled into a corner of the sofa. "I'll be able to run my ranch and do things my way and…and there won't be anyone else around to argue with me or tell me what to do—or accuse me of having hormone problems." Or to make love to her, grin at her with brilliant blue eyes sparkling with possessive delight, discuss cattle breeding and new methods of ranching or even just hold her hand.

She finished her tea, rinsed the mug and wandered into her bedroom, switching off lights as she went. She stopped at the door of her room and frowned at the interior. The room seemed too small and too empty, and there wasn't much inviting about her lonely bed. She sank onto it. Okay, maybe she had become a little accustomed to being with Morgan. Right now, being all alone didn't seem too appealing, but that was simply because of all today's excitement. Tomorrow, she'd feel differently. Tomorrow, this aching loneliness would go away and so would the accompanying sensation of loss. She was glad she didn't have to get married although she felt badly for Morgan. *I've probably been in love with you for some time,* he'd said. *But you don't feel the same way about me.*

"I'm not going to think about Morgan," Lacy muttered. "I'm going to think about that silver mine and running this place by myself."

She crawled into bed and closed her eyes. This had turned out pretty much the way Sarah Larkspur's life had turned out. Jake had ridden in to save her, then had disappeared into the sunset. Morgan had done the same thing. He'd saved her ranch for her. And he'd done the modern-day equivalent of riding off into the sunset.

She had gotten what she wanted—the same way Sarah had gotten what she wanted. Of course, Morgan had said that Sarah wasn't too smart.

Lacy opened her eyes, switched on the light and sat up in bed. Morgan was right. Sarah hadn't been very clever. Maybe she could have had Jake Malone, but she'd chosen not to. Instead, she'd spent her entire life alone. No matter how much Lacy told herself that was what she wanted, the truth was that she didn't. She wanted to amalgamate properties and buy a fridge and move into Morgan's house and turn it into a home and get a whole bunch of those little Japanese cattle.

Most of all, she wanted Morgan.

MORGAN SAT IN HIS KITCHEN, trying not to think about the pain in his ribs. Talk about uncomfortable—and he hadn't even taken a bullet. To think his brother did this for a living. He'd always wondered about Wade's choice of profession. This episode had convinced him once and for all that Wade was crazy.

He shifted around in the chair, trying to find a comfortable position. Pain had kept him awake most of the night—and it wasn't just the bullet, either. There was another pain in his chest that had nothing to do with his injury. That one was Lacy's fault. He squeezed his eyes at another painful jolt. He could just picture her in here, teasing him, ripping off his clothes, arguing with him about how to run the place. Damn but they would have had a good life together. He could almost see the kids they would have had—a couple of boys, one like him and one with no sense like his brother. A girl like her and maybe one like Rita. A real home, just like other folks had.

But that wasn't about to happen. Morgan got to his feet. He was going to have that someday. He just wasn't going to have it with Lacy. And right now, all he wanted was Lacy.

He heard the sound of a pickup pulling into the yard. Lacy's truck. She must be here for her horse. He grimaced. The last person he needed to see today was Lacy. Maybe she'd go right to the corral and...

But she didn't. He was starting toward the window to check it out when she burst through the door, hair flying, eyes sparkling. She stopped dead when she saw him and gave him a tentative smile. "Hi, Morgan."

"Morning, Lacy," Morgan said, striving for a casual tone. God, he loved her. He loved everything about her, from the way she looked in a pair of jeans to the freckles on her nose.

"How are you feeling?"

There weren't enough words in the dictionary to describe that. "Not too bad," Morgan muttered. "You're here for that horse of yours, are you?"

"Forget the horse," Lacy interrupted. "I'm not here for that. I'm here for dynamite."

"Dynamite?"

"Uh-huh." She glanced around the kitchen as if she expected to find a stack of it piled near the coffeemaker. "Do you have any?"

"I might have a little left over from when I—"

"Good." She started out the door. "Let's go get it."

Morgan put a hand on her arm and turned her to face him. "Now just hang on there, Lacy. What in tarnation do you want with dynamite?"

"I want to blow something up, of course."

She acted as if he should know what she was talking about. Morgan replayed every conversation he'd had with her—and drew a blank. "What is it you want to blow up?"

She crossed her arms and looked him square in the eye. "That silver mine."

Oh, God, it was another hormone thing. "You're going to *what?*"

"I'm going to blow it up." Her eyes flashed. "I'm going to blow it up real good, Morgan, so that no one will ever be able to tell it was there."

Morgan reached up a hand to scratch behind his left ear. "I don't think you want to do that."

"Oh, yes, I do." She shoved her hands into her pockets. "Before we knew there was a silver mine on our property, you were going to marry me. Right?"

"That's right."

"Then I'm going to get rid of it." She compressed her lips and straightened her shoulders, her entire body emanating determination. "Then I'll be broke again. And do you know what that means? It means you'll *have* to marry me."

Morgan gaped at her.

"You'll have to," Lacy went on breathlessly. "If you don't, I'll lose the ranch and have to move into town and work as a teller. And I'm terrible with money. The whole town will go broke."

"What the hell?"

"I'll probably get fired. I've never worked anywhere besides the ranch and I don't expect to be good at it. My parents will nag me and I'll have to go to the city to find someone to marry just to get them off my case. And that would be a real shame. I don't want to marry someone else. I want to marry you."

Morgan shook his head. The woman had definitely gone off her rocker. "We've already had this discussion."

"No, we haven't. You had the discussion. You told me I wasn't in love with you, and I believed you. But you're wrong. I am."

"Now, Lacy—"

Lacy stomped her foot. "Don't you 'Now, Lacy' me. I'm trying to tell you that I love you. I want to spend the rest of my life with you. I want to amalgamate our properties and fill this house with kids and buy a new fridge and I don't even care if I start doing abnormal things like making oatmeal cookies with raisins in 'em and using your name in every sentence. I'll even learn to sew if that's what you want."

Morgan couldn't think of a thing to say. He just stood where he was, staring at her.

"I don't know how I'm supposed to look at you," Lacy went on desperately. "I practiced in front of the mirror all morning, but I'm not sure I've got it right. I think I look at you the way I've been looking at you all my life. Like you're the most handsome man on the continent. The smartest. The bravest. The kindest. You're the man of my dreams, the man I want to spend my life with, and I was a darn fool not to realize it a long time ago."

Morgan's gaze swept her face. And there in her green eyes was the look he'd been waiting all this time to see.

"Will you marry me?" she asked.

Morgan had to swallow twice to get rid of the lump in his throat. Still, his voice, when he spoke, was rough and raspy. "If that's what you want...yes."

"It is." Lacy leaped up and threw her arms around him. He kissed her again and again while she wriggled and squirmed against him as if she never wanted to let him go. Finally, they had to come up for air. Lacy burrowed her head into his shoulder and nibbled at his ear while he kept both arms wrapped around her. "Morgan," she whispered.

"Hmmm?"

She rotated her hips against his. "That's not all I want."

"Me, neither," Morgan growled. He swooped her up and started for the stairs with her clinging to him.

When they reached the bottom step, Lacy put a hand on his chest and raised her head. "Wait a minute. What about your ribs? How are they?"

Morgan had forgotten all about them. "A mite sore."

"Oh." Lacy snuggled her head against his shoulder and took a long suck on his earlobe. "In that case, I guess we'll just have to be careful."

Morgan smiled and pulled her higher and closer, hardly daring to believe his luck. She was here, and she was his. "Whatever you say, Lacy. Whatever you say."

A FEW HOURS LATER, Lacy stood on the sloping ground and watched as Morgan shoved the last bundle of dynamite into a rock crevice. "Are you sure you know what you're doing?"

"Nope." He brushed his hands together to remove the dirt. "I'm making it up as I go along."

"Morgan!"

He grinned at her, a wide, face-splitting grin, and his eyes sparkled with laughter and endless love. "I'm just teasing you, honey. I know exactly what I'm doing."

Of course he did. Morgan knew everything. She rolled her eyes at the thought. There she went, turning into Janice. She smiled again. It wasn't that bad a feeling.

Morgan's grin slipped away. "What about you? You're blowing up a whole pile of money here. Are you sure *you* know what you're doing?"

"I know exactly what I'm doing. I talked it over

with my parents, and none of us wants this place turned into a major silver mine. And I don't care about the money." She slid an arm around his waist and looked up at him. "As long as I've got you, I'll be happy. But what about you? Do you mind? I mean, the money would've been ours."

"I'm not anxious to have a mine operating down here, either." Morgan pressed his lips against her temple. "All I ever wanted was you, Lacy. You know that."

Lacy caught her breath at the love in his eyes. "Then let's get on with it."

Morgan handed her the detonator. "It belongs to you. I think you should be the one to do it."

"All right." Lacy took one last look at the silver mine. Then she slowly lowered her thumb and pressed the button. There was an instant of silence, then a thunderous noise as rocks came crashing down the hillside to land in front of the entrance, sealing it forever. They stood in silence, watching the dust settle. Then Lacy took Morgan's hand and tugged him toward the horses. "Let's go home. I need to check your ribs."

"Right." Morgan grinned down at her. "Although sometimes I get the feeling that it isn't my ribs you're interested in, honey."

"You might be right." As she pulled him along, she took a quick glance over her shoulder and froze.

A man was standing beside the fallen rocks a hundred yards away. He was over six feet tall, with a brown mustache and an unshaven chin. He was wearing brown pants, tucked into high-scuffed boots, brown leather chaps and a dusty-looking brown oilskin.

As she watched, he tipped his hat to her, then turned and moseyed off into the trees.